BLOODSHOT

Bloodshot
(Blood Rights, Book Five)

K. B. Thorne

Bloodshot Copyright © 2020 by K. B. Thorne
Originally Published as *Disposable People* by Mia Darien, 2014

All Rights Reserved.

No part of this book may be reproduced or transmitted in any form
or by any electronic of mechanical means, including photocopying,
recording or by any information storage or retrieval system, without
the written permission of the publisher, except where permitted by law.

No part of this book may be used to train AI.

This book is a work of fiction. Names, characters, places, and incidents
either are the products of the author's imagination or are used
factiously, and any resemblance to actual events or persons, living or
dead, is entirely coincidental.

ISBN: 979-8-9929722-9-0

Printed in the United States

This story is dedicated to my husband, who will forever and for always be the Vance to my Sadie.

CHAPTER ONE

Everything is kind of foggy now, but I think I remember most of it. There are some spots that aren't clear, and some that I even doubt my memory. You'll understand when I get there, but I'll try to be the best narrator I can. I've always tried to be the best I can be at everything I do, and when telling a story as personally important as this, I think it's particularly important, right?

I'll go back to the night I felt this story really began. Like most stories, it started before it started. Things led up to things that led to other things before we reach the point, so bear with me.

Well, first off, my name is Vance Johnston. I am a detective for the Adelheid Police Department. The night it began started with me running through the woods. This wasn't unusual. I ran through the woods a lot, because I needed to. The tiger within was desperate to get out from time to time and stretch its legs. When you're a weretiger, see, these are the types of things you need to do.

So, I was out for a run that night. It wasn't the full moon or anything, just a bit of exercise. I wasn't alone, either. Madison was with me, because she's a werewolf, so her wolf liked to come out and play with me when I hit the tree line. She's practically my sister now anyways, even if not by blood. (Cats and dogs, right?) She's sort of dating a weretiger, though, so she obviously doesn't mind us cats, and I know she likes me. She only threatened to tear me to shreds once, and that had nothing to do with me but with Sadie, my girlfriend at the time and Madison's roommate, best friend, and boss. The threat was, as I recall, if I ever hurt Sadie that Madison would tear me into pieces small enough to eat, starting with somewhere...well, somewhere very sensitive.

At the time, I laughed and said something about her wolf. She said not as a wolf, and I took her seriously. I would never hurt Sadie anyways, but I appreciated Madison's sisterly affection for her.

Anyways, we were out for a run. One tree looks like another, but it was nice to let the beast out to get some air. We sprinted full bore through the woods, not racing but sort of racing. Unacknowledged competition, if you will. I was winning, because my body and legs are longer and I chew up a lot more ground per stride than her, but she was making a very good effort. She was fast.

We both skidded to a very abrupt halt when a smell crossed our path. There was an animal nearby. It was a little one. A rabbit. We must have been upwind of it because it would have been long gone otherwise when a wolf and a tiger came crashing in its direction. Come to think of it, the sound alone should have done it, so I'm still not sure what the critter was doing there, but there it was.

Suddenly realizing its danger, it finally darted out and went rushing away from us.

Madison's wolf began to go after it, excited for the chase, but I blocked her body with my own like the orange and black stripes were the bars of a gate.

Having no language, she cocked her head as her lupine eyes looked at me, and I swung my large head back and forth. She took my meaning. Not looking too happy about it, mind, but she got my meaning and followed me when I took off loping in a different direction. Let the rabbit be, I figured. It was probably gonna have a little bunny heart attack after seeing the pair of us anyways.

We ran for a while longer. I guessed it was about an hour, but since tigers have neither watches nor cell phones, I couldn't be sure. We completed a circuit and headed back to where we had stashed our clothes, which was a small copse of trees providing a semblance of privacy where we shifted back into our human forms.

The change between animal and human is always a frightening thing, even if you'd been doing it at least once a month (full moon) since puberty. (Werecreature children get an extra perk at an already awkward time of life.) Bones and joints pop and crack as they shift, and muscles make this kind of sickly stretching sound. It hurts like hell, too. But it only lasts a minute, and you kind of get used to it.

Once back in human form, we put our clothes on. See, the change does not include anything on your body, so say farewell to any clothes you're wearing if you change while wearing them. Nudity isn't a big deal to werecreatures, however, probably thanks to our inner animals, so it wasn't a big deal that we shifted around each other.

"Why'd you stop me going after the rabbit?" she asked, fastening her bra. "I wasn't going to hurt it. I don't like live prey. You know that."

"I do," I agreed, sliding my belt through the loops of my jeans. "But there was no reason to scare it more than it already was."

She shrugged. "Can't hurt to give the animal a little fun sometimes. It's in our natures, after all."

"Maybe, but we don't have to indulge in all of our beastly selves. The run through the forest should be enough."

"Fine, fine," she said.

I pulled on my t-shirt and then my jacket. It was April, but it was Connecticut and convincing warmth was still a ways off. When I pulled my jacket from the ground, however, something tumbled out of the pocket. I didn't realize it until

Madison got a hold of it, her eyes lighting up like a kid at Christmas.

"What is this?" she asked with the biggest damn grin ever. She held a small, red velvet jewelry box. The grin grew impossibly wider as she went on, "Is this what I think it is? Is it? Is it?" She was practically bouncing, and you'd have thought it was for her.

"Yes," I admitted, because there was no lying now.

She squealed, literally squealed, and opened it. Inside was a white-gold-banded ring with a garnet heart surrounded by tiger's eye. She tilted her head. "Isn't it supposed to be a diamond? A skating rink?"

I snatched it back out of her hand. "It's supposed to be what fits the woman," I replied, a touch annoyed. "Her favorite stone is garnet."

She grabbed it back. "And she loves listening to your heartbeat," she said, catching on. My girlfriend was, after all, a vampire. She always had an affinity for listening to my heart work, because she missed having one of her own. "And tiger's eye." She smiled apologetically and handed it back. "It's beautiful." Pause. "Why are you carrying it around tonight?"

I all but scuffed the toe of my shoe in the dirt. "I've had it for weeks. I just haven't gotten the guts to do it."

She smacked my arm like a little sister. "Why not?!"

"Because," I replied, pushing her away but in a friendly manner, "she's a vampire, and I know she gets weird about the forever thing. You know? I'm not. I don't know if she'll think it's a good idea."

"Oh," she said, frowning thoughtfully. "Cameron was a werewolf, and she wanted forever with him."

Cameron St. John. Madison's brother, and the man responsible for Cameron's Law, making all us freaks legal to be ourselves in the United States.

"Yeah, and…" I stopped. I didn't like saying it to her, even if it was years ago.

"He died," she said it for me. "Right. You're afraid she's going to say no because she doesn't want to see you die before her. I get that, but she's already with you. She loves you. I don't think she intended to get into a relationship with you just to break up with you when you started showing signs of getting old. She's not like that. She would've gone after another vampire if that was the case."

I closed the box and stuffed it back in my pocket. "Rationally, I know that, Madison, but this isn't a rational matter."

She moved beside me and put her head on my shoulder. "It's not, because you love her and she loves you. So you should get married and move in." She poked me in the side. "But you're not kicking me out. You'll be legally stuck with me!"

I laughed, because I couldn't help it. She always had that effect on me. "I wouldn't dream of even trying. Okay, I'll ask. Just don't say anything to her about it."

"Steal all my fun," she said with a mock pout. "But fine. Do it soon, though. I don't know how long I can hold this in!"

Laughing again, I pushed her off me. We put on the last of our clothes and shoes, and just as I was getting my car keys out of my pocket, my cell phone rang.

"Johnston," I answered, holding a hand up for her to wait a moment. My new partner was on the other end.

"You available to come to work?" she asked.

"Sure. What's going on?"

"Undercover weapon sale gone wrong. Paranormal elements. I'm already on scene, and we're just waiting for your charming company."

I groaned. I was technically just on my lunch hour, after all, but still. I'd hoped to go back to the station so I could work through the Mount Everest of paperwork that had accumulated on my desk.

"Let me just drop Madison back at the office and I'll be right there."

She gave me the address, and we headed to my car.

Chapter Two

After dropping Madison off, I headed straight to the address. It was deeper into downtown Adelheid, to a section considered less than savory, shall we say. It's not the biggest of towns, but every city has its dark side. I got to see all of them, thanks to my job.

I parked at the end of the line and made my way to the alley where all the action was. I didn't have to flash my badge because everyone knew me. My new partner came out under the streetlight to greet me.

"Have a good run?" she asked.

"Until you called." But I smiled.

Detective Samantha Moore, human psychic with the skill of psychometry, which is the reading of impressions, emotions, and history from inanimate objects. Recently transferred from Hartford, CT. We had been together about a month by this point. I had known her before, though, because we worked on something together a while back. So I knew her and liked her, knew she was competent, though it always took time to work out the kinks of a new partnership.

She led me into the alley, although as soon as I'd gotten near it, I could smell smoke and something like...cooked meat?

What the hell...

"Let me introduce you to today's contestants," Sam began, leading me to a pair of charbroiled bodies. "This is

Frankie Motts and Greg Wallman." She gestured to a body with each name, but then paused. "Or the other way around. Hard to tell. Anyways, two small-time weapons dealers looking to get into the bigs." She folded her arms across her chest, making her brown leather jacket crinkle. "They were trying to make a deal with a lowbie in the Blackwood Family." She paused and let that sink in.

Both my brows shot up. "Blackwood?" I repeated. Not being in the FBI's organized crime division, I didn't know all the dirt. But the Blackwood Crime Family was very well known to all law enforcement, a mob of the old school before the mob, led by a family of vampires. Yeah, it's a new day. They were into every crime, paranormal and not, that you could think of.

Once Sam watched that information stop rolling through my eyes, she went on. "We got to them first, and apparently they agreed to let us put this meeting under surveillance, so we could climb the ladder. They were meeting with a guy that goes by the street name of McGrath, though we don't know anything else."

"So, what happened?" I asked, pointing to the smoldering corpses.

"McGrath is, apparently, electrokinetic."

It's about what it sounds like. Like a telekinetic can move things and a pyrokinetic controls fire, an electrokinetic can manipulate electricity.

"Somehow, he knew. He fried them and when the team moved in, he zapped them too. Fortunately, he only knocked them out for a few minutes so he could escape. Whether it was a lack of time or he didn't want to kill cops, I don't know, but those guys are fortunate, at least." Back on the other side of the alley, I saw five cops looking rather sore and out of it.

One of them broke off and approached us. This was a young woman. She was fairly small with a Hispanic cast to her face, but I sensed she was preternatural instantly, so I knew her size said nothing of her strength and speed. I then noticed she was wearing only half her uniform, pants and boots but a white t-shirt.

"Officer Julia Diaz," she introduced herself with a formal nod. "I was the lead on the surveillance. I was positioned on the edge of the rooftop—" She pointed to the building on our left. "—in falcon form with a recording device on my leg sending the surveillance feed back to the van." Okay, that explained the uniform. It was what she'd been given after shifting back.

"Are you all right?" I asked, genuinely concerned. "Were you caught in the electric knockback?"

She smiled politely. "I was, but I'm fine. Thank you, sir. The recording has already been brought back to the station."

With a nod and polite smile of my own, I let her go back to the paramedics and other officers. Sometimes being preternatural could come in handy, I thought, like falcons with recording devices.

"What else do we know?" I asked Sam.

"Motts lived alone and no family we know of. Wallman had a live-in girlfriend."

I watched as two folks from the medical examiner's office managed to transfer the bodies to black bags for transport back to the morgue. Uniformed officers continued combing the scene for any extra clues, but I knew what our next stop needed to be.

"Let's go tell his girlfriend," I said wearily. This was always the part I hated. "Do we have a name?"

Sam looked at her notebook. "Penny Wilcox."

We went to the car. Sam had the address, but I did the driving. Maybe it was a typical guy thing, I don't know, I just preferred to drive. She didn't seem to mind, so we went with it.

About ten minutes later, we reached a series of

apartment buildings just on the outside of downtown. The place we wanted was a bottom-floor apartment with faded, chipped green paint on the door and the C in 1C hanging upside-down. I knocked.

"Who is it?" a woman's voice called from the other side.

"Police," Sam replied. I let her do the talking because I knew when a woman was answering the door and likely alone, a woman's voice was less intimidating.

There was a long silence, and I wondered if she'd gone out the back window.

"Ms. Wilcox," Sam called with another knock.

After another long pause, the door opened the length of her burglar chain. Sam and I both held up our badges.

"What do you want?" the woman asked with uncertainty in her dark eyes.

"May we come in?" Sam asked. "I'm afraid we have some bad news about Greg Wallman."

Dark brows drew together. "What's happened now?" she asked, but something in her expression told me she already knew. She didn't wait for an answer before opening the door and ushering us into a living room that smelled like cigarettes and had nothing more than a threadbare red couch and a small television set.

It was my turn. Sam was better at these things than my last partner, but I'd gotten in the habit of being the one to deliver bad news.

"I'm sorry, Ms. Wilcox, but Greg was killed tonight." There was no way to put that nicely, so I went for it straight.

She didn't start crying, but they didn't always. Shock took a lot of them first, which kept them silent, or in denial. Some got angry. I'd fielded a punch or two in my day. She was quiet, but deflated.

"He went and did something stupid this time, didn't he?"

"We're still piecing things together," I replied. Until we knew more, she didn't need to know all the gory details. "Do you know what he was doing tonight?" She bit her bottom lip and hesitated. "You won't be in any trouble."

She still considered it for a few moments before saying, "Yeah, he was going to sell a few guns. He does that. He said there were big things going on, but he wouldn't tell me anything about it."

Without any better idea she did actually know something, I wasn't keen to interrogate a woman who'd just suffered a loss. So, we gave her the usual information, and I gave her my card to call if needed. Unlike most, she didn't ask for details about what happened. Which was slightly odd, but not suspiciously so. Many don't want to know right away, but I imagined we, or the ME, would be hearing from her soon.

We went to the station.

CHAPTER THREE

The car ride had been relatively quiet, since neither of us was feeling particularly cheerful. One never really does after a notification of someone's death. It's just depressing, but it's part of the job. And this one had been quieter than most. Telling a parent a child has died is always the hardest, but telling anyone their loved one isn't coming home again is bad. I wasn't going to spend much time thinking about it, though. It would just depress me further.

Once we were back at the station, a young man in uniform—he was new and I didn't know his name yet—greeted us in the squad room and told us the surveillance footage was ready to be viewed. I thanked him namelessly and then went to Sam's desk, where she was already sitting and getting things rolling. All I had to do was sit down and watch.

The alley was empty, and we watched until we saw two men walk in. Since Officer Diaz had been on the rooftop, we mainly saw the tops of their heads, but I knew it to be Motts and Wallman. They lingered for a while, fidgeting and looking like two people up to no good. This could explain why they hadn't yet made it into the big time and had been picked up before even having the chance.

By the time I came back from the breakroom with two cups of coffee, a third man (McGrath) had finally shown up. They started talking about guns that had been magically enhanced. It was the newest thing. After enhanced drugs came the weapons.

It was pretty standard, talking money and merchandise, until McGrath reached into his pocket and took out his phone. He stepped away and spoke too quietly for the camera to pick it up, glancing back at the two men a couple of times before putting the phone away.

Returning to Wallman and Motts, McGrath tilted his head. I couldn't see his expression, but I could clearly hear him say, "Looks like the year of the rat just got a little longer." Before extending both hands and shooting bolts of electricity into the men. The power was so strong, it was like a flash of lightning. The men seized and fried. We didn't get the whole show on that one as the camera was already shaking with the officer's movement.

Diaz let out a piercing avian shriek before swooping off the ledge and I could see four cops pouring in from the end of the alley. McGrath's face stared up at the falcon coming his way and then a burst of light and...

Nothing. The camera died. If not for the wireless feedback to the nearby van keeping the recording, we never would've gotten this.

Sam leaned back in her chair and then spun around to look at me. Her gray-green eyes were narrowed thoughtfully.

"It's the year of the snake," she finally said.

Leaning back against the desk, I met her gaze. I had absolutely no idea about Chinese astrology, so I was more than happy to take her word for it.

"Year of the rat," I said. "Rat... Someone tipped him off that Motts and Wallman had been turned."

"That's what I'm betting," she said. Looking over her shoulder at her desk, she pulled up three folder files. "And looks like we got another present while we were away. Here are the files on Motts, Wallman, and what little is known about this guy McGrath." She handed one to me. I had Motts.

I began reading. "Nothing exceptional," I commented after a few minutes. "He was in and out of trouble starting in high school, a few days here and there in jail but nothing serious until after he missed graduation. Then we have a couple stints in prison, but nothing over eighteen months. No paroles, however. He always did the full term. Drugs and guns. That's his whole pedigree."

"This one too," Sam said. "Although he's got an attempted armed robbery charge, but the case didn't stick. Witness recanted. Otherwise, not all that much here." She paused and frowned. "How would these two guys ever get in touch with someone on the Blackwood radar?"

"That is a very good question," I said. "What do we have on McGrath?"

She opened that file. "Very little. He's never been arrested, so all we have is information associated with him and suspected. I bet we only have the file because of his ties to Blackwood, which our information on in here is limited at best. Electrokinetic, we already know that. McGrath is just his street name. Everything says he only deals in weaponry." She tossed the folder back onto her desk. "So, nothing at all, really."

Shaking my head, I handed my file back to her to keep them together.

The phone rang, and I answered it. It was Dr. Cor down at the office of the medical examiner.

"Detective," he greeted me. "We haven't conducted the full autopsy yet, but we have taken dentals and confirmed the identity of the two victims."

"Thanks, doc," I replied. We already knew since we had them under surveillance, but I didn't say anything to him about that. "Let us know if you find anything interesting when you get to the autopsies." And I hung up. I liked Cor. He was a competent ME, but he was also twelve. (Okay, exaggerating, but he was very young.)

"Your favorite ME calling to tell you what you already know?" Sam asked, eyeing me over the rim of her coffee cup.

"Yeah," I replied.

"I think he's got a crush on you." She grinned.

If it wouldn't have been childish, I might have thrown something at her. "Too bad for him. I'm already taken." I paused. "Speaking of which, what happened with you and—"

She cut me off. "I don't want to talk about it."

I wasn't going to push the issue. (I kept trying, though.)

We sat down to do some paperwork and about an hour into that, we were told we had a guest. I looked up to see a man in a dark suit with a big smile walking toward me, and I smiled back.

"Agent Lang," I said, getting up to shake his hand. "It's been a while."

"It has. How're you doing, Detective Johnston?" His look was pointed, and I laughed.

"Fine, Jackson. How're you?"

"I'm good, Vance." He turned to Sam. "And who is this?"

I remembered I had manners. "Right, this is my new partner. I'm sure you've heard about her."

He nodded and offered his hand to her next. "Of course. Detective Moore, right?"

"Yes," she said politely. "You're with the FBI. You worked with Vance and his last partner on the Novel Killer case."

Jackson winced. "I hate that name, but yes, I did."

I sat back down and looked at him curiously. "What brings you by? No more serial killers, I hope."

"No." He shook his head. "It's actually because of your case tonight. It pinged at headquarters. I was already in the area, so they asked me to stop by."

I had a good idea why he'd been in the area, but I didn't say. "The FBI must be here because of Blackwood."

He made that slightly obnoxious 'you got it' gun motion, but I kept that feeling to myself. "Our organized crime division has been after that fish for a while. I'm not going to say vampires are smarter than everyone else, but I am going to say they are better at hiding things. This is a slippery group to get a tag on. We have lots of rumors and speculations, and what seem like some good leads, but nothing to bring a charge."

"Are these vampires filing their taxes?"

"No Al Capone this time," Jackson said with a wry smile.

Sam smirked.

"I'm here to give you a quick tutorial, and then ask in my nicest inter-governmental agency cooperation voice that you let us know if your investigation actually pops on Blackwood at all."

"For you, Jackson, anything," I said.

"This is why you have all the boys chasing you," Sam murmured wickedly, and I glared at her. Jackson either didn't hear or very convincingly pretended he hadn't.

"We'll start at the beginning, lady and gent," Professor Lang began. "The Blackwood Crime Family is slippery because while professional criminals can be tough enough, it's even harder when you're dealing with vampires. As far as we know, the patriarch—Alastair Blackwood—was born in Scotland sometime in the early eighteen hundreds. He was already well into adulthood, married with three nearly grown children, or the 'nearly' by today's standards, late teens and early twenties. Pretty much adults in that day. He was turned sometime in his forties. We don't know anything about his sire, but we know he was obviously a bastard early on, because the first things he did after that was kill his wife and turn all three kids."

"This guy sounds like a real sweetheart," Sam drawled.

Jackson smirked. "I know. Sounds like a criminal,

right?" He continued, "We don't know much about them after that, but they seemed to work on the vampire thing and reemerged about a hundred years later as the new up-and-coming in crime."

I thought about it. "Early nineteen hundreds. Vampire magic would make that a walk in the park."

"Precisely," Jackson agreed. "So while we know they were around and up to no good, and a real family business at that, we don't know a lot. We know they emigrated from the UK to the United States in the thirties and made the most of the Great Depression.

"After Cameron's Law, however, they've come out of the shadows. They've jumped onto every magic-enhanced illegal enterprise possible and have been rapidly expanding their territories. However, this means we've learned a lot more about them in the past few years."

"But not enough to make an arrest stick, obviously?"

"Obviously." He ran a hand through his hair, though it never seemed to move. "We were able to follow a lead enough to put a man undercover."

That got the brows up on both Sam and I. "And?" I prompted.

He looked uncomfortable there. "We've lost contact." He paused for a sigh. "He hasn't gotten in touch with his handler in a couple of weeks."

"Any chance he's gone quiet to avoid being found out?" Sam asked.

"There's a chance, so we're not hitting the panic button yet, but we're getting worried. He was normally very on top of keeping in touch. So, when I saw your case tonight come over our radar with a possible Blackwood connection, you can understand why I jumped on it."

"Certainly," I agreed. "We have nothing right now, though. All we have is a gun buy gone very wrong, two fried bodies, five dazed cops, and a guy with a street name of McGrath on the run."

"McGrath," Jackson repeated thoughtfully. "I've heard that name before. Yeah, definitely connected to Blackwood, though I don't know how high up the ladder."

"Can't be too high if he was sent to meet Motts and Wallman," Sam pointed out. "They were pretty small time and even if they found an in, that wouldn't mean they'd rate a top lieutenant, you know?"

Jackson and I nodded.

"So, you'll let me know if you find anything?" he asked. I nodded again. With a smile, he thanked us and started out. "Got someone waiting on me." He flashed a knowing look in my direction and then was out the door.

"Love it when the feds stop by," Sam quipped as she turned back to her desk.

"Jackson is a good guy," I said. "Though I'm sorry his partner wasn't with him, or here instead. I would kill for you to steal her pen or something and tell me more about her."

She whirled to face me with a dry smirk. "I thought you already had a girlfriend with her, ahem, teeth in you."

I was not amused. "Not like that," I retorted. "She's just a preternatural species I can't figure out for the life of me. Doesn't smell like any species I've ever known, and she's not fessing up. With your abilities, I could cheat."

Sam laughed, shook her head, and turned back to her computer.

Chapter Four

The work night ended surprisingly quietly. No more leads on our case, but a promise of the autopsy report by the time we started our next shift. No other dead bodies decided to pop up before I could go home.

Although I didn't actually go home. I went to Sadie's. Madison was out, so it was a nice change to have the house to ourselves.

'Dinner' is always a unique affair when you're in love with a vampire. It consisted of food on one side and a glass of suspiciously thick red wine on the other, but it was fine.

"How was work?" she asked as we sat down at her half-sized dining room table. It was a good size for short little women like Sadie and Madison, but I felt like an ogre.

"The usual. Dead people." I grinned.

"You'd think you'd get enough of that at home." She grinned back, which flashed the pointy teeth, and then took a long sip of her liquid meal.

I rolled my eyes and began eating. Steak. Cat needed meat. "And the office?"

She waved a hand. "I'm still looking for an animator. I interviewed a couple today. One might be okay. The other was a sideshow. Madison should screen those, but I think she lets one through every now and then to punish me for something."

I had to laugh at that. 'Side show' usually meant they

were worthy of Vaudeville or a circus fortune teller tent, with likely not an ounce of ability to raise the dead.

"I miss Sarah," Sadie complained. "She was fantastic."

"Of course she was fantastic," I agreed. "That's why her amazing animator abilities blossomed into full-blown necromancy and necessitated her leaving to get better training. If she hadn't been that fantastic, she'd still be working for you and not off at some crazy school in Europe."

She made a face. "I know. I'll find someone."

Sadie had the pleasure of owning her own business, which meant that she could work any eighty hours a week that she wanted for very little money. Actually, she did okay on that score, but she still worked a lot.

The Stanton Agency had been up and running for a few years now, started after Cameron's Law as a way to help the preternatural and human communities interact, but also to offer specialized paranormal services. Presently, she employed a bounty hunter that specialized in preternatural beings and a demon summoner/lawyer team, and a guy who worked some IT but was otherwise a bodyguard for the animator she didn't have anymore when the anti-preternatural crowd was harassing her. He'd go to the next one, when one was hired.

Madison was the night secretary. Given it was a business that worked after dark, the day secretary was really just an answering machine.

"Oh," Sadie said, setting down her glass. "Edward and Dakota have a closing date for that property."

I grinned. "That's awesome. Lorelei planning her move now?"

She nodded. "Looking at box trucks and everything."

Okay, that's another reference that needs explanation. I mentioned that the office had a bounty hunter: Dakota, the most crabby, sarcastic, pain in the ass shapeshifter you'll ever meet, but one who's really not that bad once you get to know her. Her brother Edward had come back into her life a year before, and he had a girlfriend in Dawe's Valley, Alabama, who he had left when he went off to find his sister.

Lorelei would be the girl. Edward didn't want to leave his sister. Lorelei didn't want to leave her dogs. She worked at a shelter and vet's office and was very devoted to it. So Dakota—see, she's really not that bad—offered to use the money she'd saved up over her long life and help them buy a big piece of rural property here in CT to set up a dog rescue, so Lorelei could help rescue the dogs being over-populated and put in shelters (or to sleep) in the south.

They had been trying to find the right place, and then working through buying it for a while now. A closing date was good news, and Lorelei would need to start planning her relocation.

"Edward is so happy that he's practically flying," Sadie said. He kind of 'worked' at the agency with his sister. More like just followed her around and tried to keep her from being a public nuisance. "Which is saying something since he's not shifting into anything with wings. Just walking on air."

"Goofy bastard," I said with no actual animosity. "Remind me to bother him about that next time I see him."

She smiled like she had a secret. "I wouldn't. Dakota is on a tear as big sister right now. She's been so annoyed that her little brother's dream and girl keep getting delayed that she's about to chew nails to make sure this goes through. You so much as look at Edward cross-eyed and you might lose your throat."

I knew if anyone could or would do it, it would be Dakota. She was a force of nature.

"Thanks for the warning," I said, but even with the dire threat, I couldn't help but chuckle. Dakota being loving was just...interesting. She had dated my new partner for a while some time back, but it hadn't worked out. Sam didn't like to talk about it and Dakota refused, so I still didn't know what went wrong.

"I really hope nothing goes wrong with this sale now that it's gotten this far," Sadie said as she and I picked up the dishes to bring into the kitchen. I helped wash, dry, and put away. "There will be bodies on the floor if anything happens at this point."

"I hope so too. I'd really hate to arrest her. She has a terrible habit of escaping custody."

After dinner and dishes, we started for the living room, but I grabbed her wrist before she got that far. I didn't really feel like watching television. I put her palm flat over my heart and let her feel it. She got that half-lidded look she always gets when I do that and led me to the bedroom.

You don't get to hear about what happened next. I'm figuring you're an adult and can figure it out, but I'm not letting you in on it.

I will say that afterward, dawn was not long in coming. When I saw the faintest hint of sun peeking around the edges of her black-out curtains, I looked at her. She smiled at me briefly before the daylight rolled her under. Vampires aren't conscious during the day, but fall into a sort of coma. It's almost like they...become dead. Like they die every dawn, just without decomposing, and wake again at dusk.

Watching the change is difficult. I had gotten used to it by that point, but it still felt strange every time. It almost felt like I was watching the last breath leave her body and for a split-second, I grieved, until I remembered that she would wake up again when the sun went down.

Still, it was a very hard thing to feel like you were seeing the one you loved die.

☾○☽

I fell asleep shortly after she did, and then woke up about noon. I didn't need a lot of sleep, must've been the cat, so six hours was more than enough. I kissed Sadie on her cold forehead and got myself together. I took a shower, got dressed, and headed out. I actually had someone to meet for lunch, so I didn't need to eat. Just took care of a few quick errands because I had the time, and then went to Molly's Diner.

Nykk Marlowe had the kind of face that you couldn't forget and was impossible to miss in a crowd. She was, ultimately, a pretty woman with a delicate face, blonde hair, and brown eyes. If her life had been any different than it had been, she may not have stood out from the usual group of women. Pretty, but unremarkable. Her adolescence had not been kind to her, however, but that's a long story and one that she's told far better herself than I ever could.

But, like I was saying, what did make her remarkable was this line of scars crawling up the side of her face. It looked vaguely like painful red ivy that started somewhere below her neckline and rose across the left side of her face until it reached her hair. It had been magic-wrought and never faded.

She smiled when she saw me, and I smiled back. She used to be my partner. I liked Sam, but I actually missed Nykk. She had always been an odd one, and a little hard to get to know, but I liked her.

Getting to her feet, she actually gave me a big hug. I froze for a moment. This was new. Therapy must be working. I hugged her back and then we sat down.

"You look great," I said, gesturing to her attractive not-police-detective attire and loose hair. I think she was even wearing make-up, though being male, I was always careful with my assumptions in those areas.

"Thank you," she said. "I feel great. I feel better than I have in a really long time."

"That's fantastic, Nykk. New job treating you well?"

She nodded.

We didn't say anything more for a moment when the waitress came by and took our orders, but then she went on. "I love it. I mean, I liked being a cop, and I do miss working with you, but advocating directly for victims who aren't dead is so much more—" She paused, looking for her word. "—fulfilling, and strangely less harrowing than working with the dead."

"That's a big change of pace for you."

"I know," she said, "but I've gotten over many of my issues of not being able to talk to victims and their families. It's more cathartic now."

I grinned and took my cup of coffee when the waitress dropped it off, drinking it black. "That's great."

She sipped her own drink. "And you? How're you?"

"I'm good. You know, life is life."

"New partner?"

"Sam's great," I began with a smile, but she didn't reply right away. She stared at me with this penetrating look, and I had visions of being in the interrogation room when she was at work. I laughed quietly and shook my head. "She is great, but it's weird. It's not the same. I miss working with you, Nykk."

She smiled more warmly than I'd ever seen. "I miss you too, Vance," she said, "but it just wasn't for me anymore. I'm sure if you give Sam a little more time, you'll feel the same about her."

I shrugged. "Probably, but I'm not always a big fan of change. It does help that I've worked with her before, back on the Rau case, so it's not like working with someone entirely new."

Nykk nodded, taking a drink of her coffee. "And Sadie?"

This made me grin outright. "That, I can speak of with more confidence," I said. "I feel like I should say I don't kiss and tell."

She gave me a dry look.

"Fine, fine. Things are really good. I mean, she's the most stubborn creature on the face of the planet..." I paused. "Scratch that, Dakota wins that one, but Sadie is close, and we have been known to butt heads, but, I mean, that kind of makes it fun too. It's been nearly two years now, so I think it's been long enough to know."

"I would think so," she agreed and looked lost in thought for a moment.

I could tell when she had something on her mind, so I asked. "What is it?"

She laughed softly. "Just thinking about romance." She met my gaze when I arched my brow. "I don't want to jinx myself, so I don't want to talk about it. But it's a...new area for me. I think I like it, though."

If she didn't want to talk about it then I wasn't going to press, but I had a very strong hunch and grinned. "Fine. But tell Jackson I said hello." I winked, and she actually *blushed*.

CHAPTER FIVE

I got into work a few minutes before five, which was when my shift started. I was cutting it a little closer than usual, but I wasn't late and that's what mattered. After my long lunch catching up with Nykk, I had a few more errands to run and, as usual, they all took longer than I had wanted or planned. For some reason, I was always stuck in the longest, slowest lines any time I went anywhere.

When I walked into the squad room, it seemed that everyone in the building was huddled around one person's monitor and were in rapt attention of whatever was on the screen. I smirked, curious as to what had them all locked up.

"Better not be porn on there," I quipped. When no one laughed, or even turned around to look at me, I knew that it was something serious and hurried forward. "What is going on?" This time, I made sure that the authority in my tone could not be overlooked. I found Sam at the middle of the huddle.

She looked up at me. "Weird-ass shit, I can say that much," she said. "Station got a tip about something bad going down somewhere. Yes, that's all they said. But they pointed us to a website, and this is what we found." She pointed to the video playing on her monitor.

I turned my gaze back to the screen and saw what seemed to be a giant stone pit, a cross between a gladiatorial ring and a post-apocalyptic scene with graffiti on the cement walls and two fighters in the middle. A faint haze hung over everything, but it didn't obscure the flashing yellow lights that circled the top.

There was an audience cheering, but I couldn't see them. The camera was on the fighters in the middle of the ring. When I first looked, they were just circling one another without attacking. Two men. Both with many injuries and covered in blood. The look they shared, however, was... frightening. I could see that even from there.

It didn't look like it could be an act. It had to be real.

I opened my mouth to speak but didn't when I saw one attack the other. The speed at which they moved was preternatural. Literally. Because the instant I saw them engage in combat, I knew they were vampires. The brief slowing of their motion that gave me a glimpse of fangs only confirmed what I could already tell. These were two vampires fighting, and they were deep, deep in blood haze.

"What the..." I trailed off as one vampire sunk his teeth deep into the neck of the other, his hands gripping shoulders and knees against the attacked one's chest. As he yanked his head back with a hunk of flesh in his mouth, they both crashed to the floor. The faint mist that had been in the air faded in an instant and something—two somethings, but too fast for me to see what they were—flew into the ring and hit each one. They immediately collapsed, obviously unconscious.

"Are the techs on this?" I had to ask.

"Yes, they're trying to trace the website's information and IP, but they can't."

"Can't?" I repeated, watching as black-masked people dragged the vampires out of the bloodied arena. "At all?"

She shook her head, sighing and looking at me. "They're hitting some kind of block that they think has to have a magico-technic component."

'Magico-technic,' a fun phrase that had to be created to explain things we were coming up against in our new world. It sounds ridiculous, doesn't it? Like something only a novelist or screenwriter could come up with, but it's an actual thing nowadays.

Cameron's Law had done a lot of good to advance our races and bring us to light, but there was a dark side. There's always a dark side. That dark side was that criminals found new ways to be criminals, and the magical and the technical were being combined, beyond the drugs and weapons I already mentioned. Like that moment, when something magical was helping to block our technical efforts to track a website.

"We're sure this is real?" I asked, even though I knew it was a stupid question when I asked it. Because I could see, I could tell, what was what.

"As best we can tell, although we know...nothing."

I was going to leave the computer and talk to Captain Roy, but then the image on the screen changed. It was still a camera on the arena, but the yellow lights stopped blinking, and red came up in their place. The sound of gates and chains echoed from off-screen before two new opponents came into the ring. One walked dejectedly while the other had to be all but carried and thrown to the floor. The black masks left, and the one on the ground scrambled to his feet.

"This is a mistake!" he screamed, turning like a trapped animal.

"Oh, fuck," Sam said suddenly.

"What?" I asked. My instincts were telling me to raise the alarm. She had just seen something new in this insane moving picture show and it was going to be bad. I just knew it.

"That's Detective Shu."

"Who?"

"Shu." She paused, grimacing when she realized her rhyme, but carried on. "Lang sent us some more information.

Detective Shu was the officer they sent undercover to sniff out the Blackwood Family. And that's him."

My brows knit hard. If I had a moment to think on it, I would've worried they had actually fused together. "Are you sure?" I asked, because this was not a good mistake to make if she wasn't 110% positive about it.

She nodded. "Yes!" She flipped through a couple files on her desk before pulling a photo out of one, holding it up in front of my face. "Don't you think?"

I looked at the picture of the officer. It was one of those formal ones in his dress blues, smiling to look confident but not so much to look goofy. That was a smile one had to work on to get perfect, but Henry Shu had managed it. I examined the planes of his face and the scar that separated one eyebrow into sections. When I looked back at the screen, I saw the eyebrow. It was him.

There was a damned undercover *police detective* in that ring, and none too happy about it.

"Go get Roy," I ordered an officer in uniform, "and someone get on the phone to the FBI." Adrenaline was surging into every cell, rushing through my bloodstream, and I was vibrating to stay in place and force myself to think clearly. "This arena has to have something to do with Blackwood, and Shu got mixed in too deep..."

"Oh god," Sam breathed. As if this hadn't all been bad enough.

On the monitor, I watched as that mist filled the arena again. Shu stopped screaming. The dejected one stopped looking dejected. They both suddenly looked enraged with the other, their eyes filling with the same bloodlust I had seen in the two vampires.

"Is Shu preternatural?" I asked.

"Yeah, he's cryokinetic."

Water and ice, I thought.

The two combatants went at each other, and it was unlike anything I had ever seen, not just physical assaults but magical ones as well. I had seen video of prides of lionesses killing prey with less violence than this. An alligator in a death roll had nothing on them either. I watched as, in barely any time at all, the one who had looked dejectedly actually *tore Shu apart* in the most vicious use of telekinesis I had never even considered.

I was a cop, and a damn tiger, but even I had to look away.

☾O☽

Jackson Lang and Posey Kai had gotten to the station fifteen minutes after we called the FBI, which meant that they had been speeding. I wondered if they had the light on too, but I didn't ask. Neither looked good for asking questions as they stormed through the squad room and went straight through Roy's open office door. I wondered if Jackson, a pyrokinetic, was on the verge of lighting everything in his path on fire, he looked so angry.

Kai... She remained a mystery to me, but I could tell that she wasn't any happier than her partner.

Now they had been in there for twenty minutes. The 'program' had been turned off so the crowd around the monitor had dispersed. Sam and I leaned against a desk with our arms crossed over our chests, watching the door for any sign of...anything. It wasn't like we could think about much else. It was hard enough when a fellow cop got killed, but when you saw it happen...and it happened *like that*? It was something else altogether.

"What are they saying in there, do you think?" Sam asked.

"No clue," I replied. "I mean, how long does it take to say

'well, this is a problem'?" I knew that was a stupid thing to say, because the FBI and our captain would have a great deal to say on this. It was a mess on so many levels. But still, I was deeply unsettled. My inner cat was growling so loud that my skin was going numb from the vibrations, and I tried not to let claws and stripes pop up.

It was rare in my life that I had such trouble keeping the beast down.

Another ten minutes passed in terse silence before the door opened. Captain Roy's broad form filled the doorframe, gesturing us inside. "Johnston. Moore."

We exchanged a quick look before hurriedly pushing away from the desk and walking into the office. Lang and Kai were standing against the far wall, looking no less angry than before.

"We have determined a course of action," Roy said, not bothering with any preamble. "We need to know what's going on with this. The Blackwood Family is..." He trailed off.

"We are going to send another undercover mission," Lang said tightly.

My head snapped around. "After what just happened to Shu? Are you insane?" I felt Moore's hand on my arm and looked down, clearing my throat. "With all due respect, that seems like a...dangerous idea."

Roy seemed tolerant of my outburst, because he didn't say anything on that and went on. "It is dangerous, but there has been more information gathered since Shu went in, and we won't be sending anyone alone."

A feminine voice floated between us, and the lilting was certainly not Sam. I turned to see Kai stepping away from the wall. "And now that we know some of what's going on, you'll be required to step out at the first hint of trouble."

"Wait," Sam said, looking around. "Did you say 'you'll' be? Like, us?"

"Yes," Roy said, but even he looked a little self-conscious about it. "We need someone not from Shu's department, and since some of the activity is in Adelheid, we are going to be involved. You also were not present at the scene of the attack on our victims yesterday. You've also both managed to keep a low profile despite our higher profile cases and not have your pictures in the paper."

Sam looked worried. I couldn't blame her. "My undercover experience is limited, Captain."

Roy looked at me. "His isn't." I didn't want to meet his eyes, but I did. "He worked narcotics for three years, prior to Cameron's Law. That was something like undercover while undercover."

I ground my teeth together. "Sir, I don't like this idea."

"I don't like it either, but we don't have a lot of time, and this is urgent. A cop has been killed in the line of duty, and we are still bound by our oaths to not only find out how that happened, but finish the job he started. Options are few. The Blackwood Family is like no other criminal enterprise. We're going to have to take risks."

Looking at my feet for a long moment, I bit back everything I wanted to say and then looked up again. "Yes, sir." My words and body were tight.

"You're going in tomorrow," Jackson said, and at least he had the good grace to look apologetic. "We'll spend the rest of your shift today in briefing."

I stepped closer to him. "If something happens to me, Nykk knows to kill you." It was in jest...sort of.

He met my gaze without flinching. "We're going to do everything we can to keep you covered, Vance," he said in a low voice.

Sighing, I nodded. But anxiety filled me at my next thought.

Oh, god. How am I going to tell Sadie?

CHAPTER SIX

By the time Lang and Kai had finished briefing us, I felt exactly not at all better about the entire situation. Sam and I agreed that it was a lousy idea and we were not thrilled about our chances for survival, but we also knew that Roy was right and that we would do our duty. If there was any chance we could find the people behind Shu's murder and help bring down the Blackwood Family, then we had to do it.

That didn't, however, make my steps up to Sadie's front door any easier. My feet felt as heavy as my heart, and as the ring in my pocket. If I was going to my doom—yes, I'm being dramatic, get over it—then it seemed wrong to propose...but then again, maybe that made it the best time?

I didn't know. My track record here wasn't really that awesome.

I knocked on her door and smelled her coming toward it. Even through the metal, I could hear her hurried steps just before she pulled it open. When she did, she smiled brightly, happy to see me. That faded very fast when she got a good look at my face, because I knew I wasn't doing very well at hiding it.

"What's happened?" she asked, fear blossoming over every feature just before she ushered me inside and shut the door.

We sat down on the couch. "I've got an assignment," I began, trying to figure out how best to say it. I looked at her face, in depth, like I was studying it for the first time. She was so beautiful. I had thought so the first time I met her, although the vampire thing at our first meeting set me back a step. I got over it fast. I couldn't resist her. Her features were strong, I guess more handsome than pretty, but it suited her. She'd had long hair when she'd died, so now it was that way forever. If she cut it, it wouldn't grow back, so she never cut it. I was okay with that, because I loved her hair.

"An assignment?" she prompted, worry still filling her eyes.

"I'm being sent undercover." I looked away and rubbed the back of my neck with a frustrated sigh. "Sam and I leave tomorrow, but I can't tell you much more than that, I'm afraid. I'm not supposed to tell anyone, you know…"

She was tugging on her bottom lip with her teeth when I looked back. I could tell that she didn't like it, but she knew she couldn't really argue. "I see," she said slowly. "Is it going to be…dangerous?"

I wasn't going to lie to her. "Yes."

Reaching out, she wrapped her hand around mine and squeezed. I appreciated that she regulated her vampire strength, though, even in her anxiety. She could break my hand if she wanted. "I don't like this. You'll be, you know, careful?"

"Of course." Leaning forward, I hugged her tight, and she hugged me back. Her grip seemed to close in more as the news sunk deeper.

"Don't die, okay?"

I laughed humorlessly. "I have no intention of doing so."

Then we just sat like that for a while. I couldn't tell her anything else about it, except how I felt. And if I told her that, it was just going to frighten her more. She hadn't been a vampire all that long, comparative to how long a vampire could live, so she still felt things like fear. (Most of them seemed to grow out of that after the first few hundred years.)

When we finally pulled apart, we didn't go far. I opened my mouth, and words just started coming out.

"You know," I began, taking both of her hands in mine as I thought about the box in my pocket, "this has got me thinking a lot about you and me." She managed a small smile for me, nodding. "About how much I love you and how it's been a great couple of years together."

"It has," she agreed, kissing me. "Didn't think I'd ever feel this way about a man again, after Cameron."

I knew that her putting me in league with him was a big compliment. I wasn't jealous of the one who came before (especially since he was actually dead). I was flattered.

"Yeah." I smiled. "So, it's got me thinking a lot about… well…about forever, I guess you'd say." I glanced down, about to go for the ring, when I looked up again and saw her face.

The look was not at all what I had expected.

It was something like…abject horror.

My words caught in my throat, and I almost hacked on them like a cat with a hairball as I tried to figure out what the hell that look could mean. We had been having a romantic moment that was about to turn into a proposal and…

What the fuck?

"What?" I asked. No way like the direct way to find something out, right?

"I can't," she replied in a gasp, shaking her head like I'd asked her to cut off her foot with a hacksaw. "I… Vance, I can't!"

"You can't marry me?!" I admit, it came out a little more angrily than it probably should have.

"What?" Confusion quickly replaced the horror. "What'd you say?"

"I was just asking about how you can't marry me?"

"Marry you?"

"Is there a fucking echo?!"

She pressed her hands over her face. "Oh my god," she moaned.

I was so confused. I threw my hands in the air, vaulting to my feet because the kinetic energy in my body just couldn't be contained anymore. The whole day had been one big snowball rolling down adrenaline hill, catching speed. "What?!" I demanded again, staring at her in alarm.

"I thought..." she began weakly, peering at me between her fingers.

"You thought *what*?" I pressed.

"I thought you were going to ask me to turn you."

I stared at her for a long few minutes while my brain tried to process everything that had happened in the past few minutes. That hadn't at all been in my mind, but now that she said it...

"And that would be a problem?"

"I've never turned anyone before, Vance, you know that," she said. "What if it doesn't work? What if you just die?"

"Well, I don't want to die, but... I mean..." I rushed my hands through my hair, gripping it tight despite it being somewhat short. "From what I understand, you don't have to actually kill me or anything. Just exchange blood, and I die, and maybe I turn or maybe I don't..."

She looked like her brain was a computer about to overheat, or an engine about to flush out steam. I couldn't put together the pieces about what the problem was in her head that the idea of it was making her brain collide with itself.

My own mind went rocketing back several years. My high school love, who I was engaged to... Until she kept pushing the wedding back, time and again, before leaving me for someone else. *Sorry, Vance, I can't spend forever with you...now that I know you're a freak.*

I stared at Sadie, feeling in the middle of a time-warp with an equally heart-crushing sensation in my chest as back then. "You're saying that spending forever with me would really be that awful," I said, not making it a question.

Not waiting for her reply, I stalked out of the house. I heard her calling after me, but I couldn't listen. The tiger was all but clawing at the surface of my skin, and it wanted *out* desperately. The anger and pain was too great. It was bleeding out of every pore, trying to rush down my skin like blood. I stuffed my hands in my pockets, pacing on her walkway while considering going back in. But I couldn't.

I gripped the ring box and pulled it out, staring at it in the palm of my hand before I threw it in the grass and rushed away.

⟪O⟫

Remember how I said at the beginning that some things are fuzzy? What happened next was one of those times. I think it was all the emotions merging with the tiger's need to get out and my need to not let it...but yeah, it is all incredibly hazy now, and I don't know really know everything that happened.

I don't think I drove anywhere, because that would've been dangerous in my condition. I know I didn't talk to Sadie or answer any of her calls. And she called a lot and left as many voicemails and texts. I ignored all of them in my supreme, self-righteous, wounded little boy temper tantrum.

Yes, I can look back at it now and know it for what it was. Know that I should have talked to her, like grown-ups do, and sorted out what the deal was, but I was pitching a fit and couldn't help it.

Somehow, I ended up on Nykk's couch. No, I wasn't so upset that I cheated on Sadie. I would never have done that no matter how upset, but Nykk was a friend and helped another friend in need. Her sister—Ana, a lovely young woman with Down Syndrome—thought it was like a sleepover and thus fun. She's low needs, but can't easily live alone so she lives with Nykk. She looks at the world with an enthusiasm that most people lose as they age. I always like being around her. She makes me feel more at ease, and I think that was true that night too. Maybe that's more why I went there, because I knew those sisters would help calm me the fuck down before I did something really stupid.

Or, at least, any stupider than I already had done.

CHAPTER SEVEN

I think I slept. I must have slept. Although 'sleep' may be too light a word for just passing out because I couldn't help it.

I woke up, or regained consciousness, pretty early in the morning. It was far earlier than I was used to, but I had to meet Sam at the station. Nykk and Ana weren't up yet, so I left a thank-you note and locked the door behind me. I stopped at Molly's and got steak and eggs, because I needed the fuel to get through the day.

There were calls, voicemails and texts from Sadie. I ignored them. I thought about calling her, but my nerves were still so ragged. Besides, it would've been a voicemail. It was daylight. She'd be dead now. And I couldn't afford to lose focus, so I'd have to have it out with her when I got back. Wasn't the best course of action, but there was no 'good' path at this point. That morning, I had a job to do. I had to do it and be as clear-headed as possible through the mist lingering in my mind.

When I got to the station, I found Sam talking to a woman I didn't recognize. She was almost as tall as me and carried herself like she'd been out of the military for all of five minutes. Sam saw me as I approached and gestured in my direction.

"This is my partner, Detective Vance Johnston," she introduced me. "Vance, this is Special Agent Lisa Warren. She was Shu's handler while he was undercover."

Okay, that made sense. I offered my hand, and she

shook it firmly. "I'd say it's nice to meet you, Agent Warren, if it were under better circumstances."

She smiled slightly. "Thank you, Detective. I can't say that Shu and I were friends, but the loss of one lessens us all."

"Well put." I inclined my head toward her.

"Shu was supposed to check in with me just over two weeks ago, but it wasn't unusual for him to be late with good cause. He had to wait for the right times, but a week overdue was strange and concerning."

The day before, Lang and Kai had briefed us on Shu's cover story, which was as liaison between Shu's fictional drug boss and the Blackwood family's drug arm. (The Blackwood Family had a lot of arms.) He had ostensibly been advocating the sale of a new drug, like heroin but infused with specific magical properties.

We were going to go in as enforcers for this fictional boss, angry that our contact had gone missing and looking for information. We'd be skating on thin ice, but it was the best course on such short notice.

"Shu was concerned that they were getting ill-tempered with him, as he put it," Warren said. "No suspicion that his cover was blown, but he was using delaying tactics to prolong his stay and not have to give them any drugs. It looks like they got tired of him, and this was their response."

"Why would they just kill him?" Sam asked. "Wouldn't they be worried about pissing off his boss?"

Warren met her gaze levelly. "The Blackwood Family worries about nothing. They are the most powerful preternatural crime organization there is right now, and they have no concern about any others. As far as we have been able to tell, and from what Shu reported, the drug business is controlled by the second son. He's a hothead, so if he got pissed, getting rid of the source of his annoyance would be nothing to him."

I inhaled slowly. "That's comforting."

Warren offered a sympathetic look. "The last he had told me, Shu was staying at that extended stay motel on West Street, since he was posing as being from California, and spent most of his time with some Blackwood associates in a business on the corner of West and Plains, which was a Blackwood front. Those are going to be your best places to start."

"Thank you, Agent." I still didn't like this. "Anything else you can tell us?"

"Watch your backs." Warren offered us each her hand in turn, we shook, and she left.

We stood in silence for a few moments, like two kids who had to tell their parents they had just thrown a baseball through a window. We looked at each other and then away and then back again.

"You're wearing yesterday's clothes," Sam commented, gesturing at my wrinkled shirt and haphazard tie. "Is everything okay? Didn't you go home last night, or at least to Sadie's?" She knew I kept clothes there.

"Long story," I replied grudgingly. "I don't want to talk about it. I have some spare clothes in back. I'll go change."

I went into the bathroom and splashed water on my face, combed my short hair with my fingers, and rinsed my mouth out. I put on the dark jeans and t-shirt I kept here, but put the jacket back on for a business casual kind of look. There wasn't a strict dress code we needed to follow, after all.

When I got back into the squad room, Sam put her hand on my arm. "Are you up for this?"

"Of course," I replied, only kind of lying. I had to be up for it, and so I would be, but that I didn't mean I *felt* up for it.

☾O☽

We got in a rental car that had been provided to us under our assumed names, from the place near the airport so it looked like we had also flown in from the west coast. It was flashier than I was used to, but not as bad as it could be.

I was quiet as we drove, at least at first. My brain was still alive with thoughts and uncertainty, filled with Sadie and doubt and hurt. I had, perhaps, been unfair to not hear her out and talk more, but it just hurt too damn bad. Worse than anything, because I am not the type to run from pain, but it was too much. We'd have a lot of shit to sort through when this assignment was over.

"Would you tell me what happened between you and Dakota?" I finally asked, because the topic of pained love was indeed on my mind.

"What's going on, Vance?" she asked, instead of answering my question.

"Things got rocky with Sadie last night." I wasn't going to admit any more than that, but it seemed only fair with the question I was asking.

She didn't press and nodded slowly. "Nothing with fireworks," she said. "Dakota is not an easy woman to handle, you know that. She's..." Sam sighed. "She's got a really good heart under all that anger and snark, and we wanted to make it work. But Hartford is an hour away, and that plus her traveling so much for her job, and just..." She shrugged. "It wasn't really much more than drifting apart. We realized it wasn't going to work."

I nodded slowly. "That was before you came here for the job, wasn't it?"

"It was," she agreed. "Don't say it. I know it sounds weird. If we weren't together, then why did I take the job here? Well, honestly, our split was painful but amicable at the same time. I do just like it here, and Hartford was... I like it better here."

"Now that you're here, do you think you guys will get back together?" I had to ask.

"I honestly don't know. Maybe, maybe not. We've been keeping our distance since I came, and she's been busy with her brother and all."

By this point, I didn't know what else to say. I wasn't even sure why I had asked, because what purpose did it serve? The issue of break-ups was on my mind, but that didn't mean her experience was anything like mine or that it would help me. After talking to her, I felt kind of bad for asking, but I wasn't sure if I should apologize for it or not. It's not like I was thinking my clearest about matters of emotion and romance.

The first place we stopped was the hotel, where the manager confirmed that 'Jerry Fan' (Shu's cover name) hadn't been there in over a week, at least. We went to the next business on the list, which was a coffee shop on West and Plains that Shu was reported to spend a lot of time at during his Blackwood business.

Behind the counter was a girl with black hair and blue eyes and way too much makeup. I showed her the picture of the 'friend' I was trying to find.

She popped her gum. "Yeah, he came in here a lot for a while." She paused, still looking at the picture. "Been a week or two, I think. Usually he'd come in, order a coffee, and wait. Someone would show up, and he'd leave."

"Paid a lot of attention to him?" I asked.

She looked embarrassed. "He tipped well."

I half-smiled. "So, you flirted?"

Pink filled her pale cheeks. "Well, yeah. I'm going to college. Can use the money."

"I ain't gonna yell at you for that," I said. Sam remained silent.

The girl smiled appreciatively when I didn't push that and handed the picture back to me. "He used to talk a lot about a sandwich shop nearby that he liked and recommended I go to. Calloway's." She gave us the address.

"Thank you," I said. Sam nodded at her, and we left.

Sam looked at me dryly. "Not all women flirt for tips, you know," she said flatly.

Now I had two women mad at me. "Yeah, but you saw the look in her eyes. You wouldn't have guessed the same thing?"

After a moment, she shrugged. "Well, yeah. Just needed to poke at you."

I didn't say anything else, started the car, and got us moving.

The next business was the sandwich shop. I was glad it wasn't an Italian place, because that would've felt a little mafia cliché.

The sandwich shop wasn't a very big one, but the smell of the cold cuts was very appealing and my inner kitty growled as we walked in. I told it to shut up.

There was a young man standing behind the counter. He smelled like a wolf shifter. They were the most common shifter in town, after all, but I bet he wasn't with the local pack. Unless he didn't know anything about what was going on in this store, but I doubted that was the case. I knew Gabriel (Adelheid's pack alpha) would never tolerate criminal activity amongst his ranks. He ran a very tight ship.

"Can I help you?" the young man asked. He sort of directed the question to me, but his eyes were latched onto Sam. I got it. She is a very striking woman.

"Yeah, we were told our friend Jerry Fan used to spend a lot of time here," I said. "We're looking for him. Does anyone here know him or know where we can find him?" I showed him the picture.

It was still the thinnest damn story I had ever heard, but sometimes the stupider it looked, the more convincing it was.

The kid finally tore his eyes from Sam and met mine. He nodded. I noticed something else in his gaze I couldn't place. I pushed that thought aside as he replied, "I remember him. He used to come in a lot with Jenna."

My brows rose. "Jenna?"

"Yeah," he said. "If she has a last name, she's never told me. But she's a student or something, comes in here to do her studying. He used to come in and sit with her a lot of the time. They'd talk, I'd guess. I didn't mind 'cause he always ordered our expensive sandwiches, and he tipped the jar well." He gestured to a glass jar with a paper taped to it that said 'tip jar' and had a few dollar bills and some change inside. That seemed to be his MO, although I wasn't gonna ask this kid if he flirted with him. I'm as open-minded as the next guy, but just didn't want to know this time. I did have to wonder if it had been smart for an undercover cop to do something to leave an impression like that.

"Maybe she can help us," Sam said. "Is there a usual day she comes in?"

"Yep." The kid nodded. "Every Tuesday, Wednesday, and Thursday, in the afternoons till evening, and then Saturday morning. Same days she's got class."

I looked at Sam. "It's Wednesday. Want to hang out a while?" She nodded, and I looked at the kid. "What time does she usually come in?"

He gestured at the tables. "Just after lunch, won't be too much longer. Can I get you food?"

We both shook our heads. "No, thanks. Not just yet."

The kid smiled, and we went to an empty table. The whole place was empty, really, but having looked at the door, I knew it had only just opened. I faced the door, and Sam and

I did our best to look like we were small talking.

"Heard of any good movies?" Sam asked with a smirk.

I chuckled. "I never go to the movies."

She tilted her head at new information. "Why not? Don't you and Sadie go on movie dates? Doesn't everyone?"

The mention of Sadie's name stung, but I ignored it. "We watch movies at home, but I never go to the theater. Makes me feel like I'm origami in those damn seats. It's hard to focus on a movie when you feel that way, so I don't even bother. We just wait till things are out on DVD or streaming online."

Sam nodded. "I love going to the movies myself."

"With that willowy body, I'm sure you fit just fine."

"I do, yes," she laughed.

Before she could say anything else, her pocket buzzed. She pulled out her phone. "I'm gonna take this outside. Be right back." Excusing herself from the table, she stepped outside and onto the sidewalk.

I sighed. Today sucked.

Getting to my feet, I went back up to the young man at the counter. I was about to order a coffee when I saw a man walk out from the room behind him. It felt wrong. I can't point to what detail told me, but dread filled me quickly. I began to take a step back, but the young man was suddenly lunging over the counter and yanking me forward. He was stronger than he looked. I would have been able to tear away from him, but the bigger one was on me by then. He reeked of werewolf as well, which meant that at our sizes and shifter selves, we were equally matched.

I opened my mouth to shout for Sam, but a fist caught me square in the lip. The taste of blood covered my tongue as I felt one of my teeth land on it.

Spitting the tooth and blood in the guy's face, I stopped trying to go backward and instead surged ahead. I leaped over the counter and drove my forehead into the kid, which put his ass on the ground. Lights out.

The big one was still a problem. I turned to take care of him and got a ham-fist to the stomach that took every ounce of oxygen straight out of my lungs. Wheezing, I slammed the heel of my foot into his toe. He grunted but brought his knee into my nose, and then I felt a needle in my neck.

I was gone.

CHAPTER EIGHT

When my eyes opened again, there was haze in front of me, and I wondered if I was outside. Then I realized the haze was in my own head and squeezed my eyes shut, waiting for it to clear. It was a bad dream. When I opened my eyes again, I'd be okay, so I opened them and looked...

Bars. Heavy, metal bars. I was surrounded in a serious cage. The tiger roared, and I didn't contain it, so I roared too. My muscles were sluggish to respond as my anger urged them to motion, but I eventually snapped through the restraint—which I was sure came from some chemical poured into my system by that needle prick—and threw my body into the bars.

The clang echoed, but it burned, and I jumped back with a hiss. Fucking magic imbued that metal, I was sure, but that didn't stop me from throwing myself into the opposite side. It burned again and didn't move at all, so I was sure the cage was anchored into the cement floor.

Dropping to the center of my imprisonment, my palms were flat against the cold cement while my shoulders bunched around my ears.

I surveyed the space beyond me and saw...more bars. I was in a cage within a cage. There were metal tables and benches lined with bodies. I smelled the lingering scent of the grave and knew there were vampires. Animals told me there were shifters. I smelled humans too, but by then, I was convinced they'd be psychics of some sorts. This room was filled with preternatural prisoners, and I was the newest inhabitant.

The tiger rebelled and whatever drug they had given me took away any hope of waking control, so I kept bouncing off the cage bars, roaring and hissing and making all kinds of awful noises my human mouth wasn't made to make but managed to anyway. I felt burns accumulating on my shoulders, which I now realized were bare because I didn't have my suit jacket or T-shirt now. I was in my jeans and A-shirt, but no socks or shoes.

My preternatural skin healed the burns fast, but the stinging and smell of burnt flesh remained.

"You shouldn't do that." A voice drifted to me from of the tables.

"Why the fuck not?!" The tiger was the one to snap. My human brain only had control of the eyes. The animal had everything else.

"Because it's pointless. You can't get out." I don't know who spoke, because they were all staring silently at metal dishes before them. I looked down and concentrated, smelling the food past the smell of persons. Meat and blood. I could smell the fat in the low-quality meat. Hopefully, it was cooked.

I snarled at the anonymous speaker.

"Suit yourself." Male, that was as much as I could tell.

Smacking my hands into the floor, I felt my nails flip back on one hand. It hurt like hell, but I didn't care. I smacked the floor till my palms were red, threatening calluses and ready to burst through the skin. I burnt my shoulders and arms on the bars some more, and no one spoke this time. They just let me have my paranormal tantrum, because there wasn't anything else I could do.

Eventually, my body wore out, and I fell again. My cheek pressed to the cement as I panted heavily.

I was so exhausted I didn't even hear the footsteps approaching until the voice spoke. I looked up from knit brows and saw a man. I inhaled slowly. Human, I could tell. I can't smell psychic abilities.

"You're just like all the others," he said. "They all think their powers will break them out of here, and yet you see all of them now...still confined for the use of our amusement, with no hope of escape. You will fall in line in time."

"Fuck you."

He smiled, and it was such a smug, vapid look. "You're just like all the others," he repeated. I felt like I should be insulted, but I didn't have the energy to be. "You will submit, just as soon as you realize this is your life now. Until it isn't."

I was about to ask how that change took place, but then I just knew. It stopped when you were dead.

I stopped looking at him. "Go away."

"You'll stay in here a while longer, until you develop a better attitude and we feel certain you can play nice with the others."

I grunted. I felt the drug in my system again now that the adrenaline was waning.

"This is what you need to remember, shifter." He wouldn't shut up. "You are here at our leisure and for our amusement. You live so long as you entertain us and make us money, and so long as you don't cause problems here in our barracks. We do not abide by troublemakers. See how all these preternatural people are behaving well together? Far better than anywhere else, even now with Cameron's Law. That's because they abide by the rules here. You abide and entertain, and you will be kept. That is the new creed you will live by."

There was a long stretch of silence, but I refused to look up. He then banged, hard, on the bars, and my nervous system couldn't help but jump.

I heard him laugh, but the sound receded and I knew he was walking away.

I closed my eyes, but I could still see the bars. I was in a cage, and it felt like those bars were closing in on me. I hated feeling confined. I didn't like small spaces. Where was I?

The man had said amusement and entertainment. I tried to think it through, so that I would stop thinking about being trapped. I had no proof, but I began to suspect that I was where Shu had been.

I was about to become a gladiator.

Outside of my cage, I could hear the dull murmur of the others talking, but no one directed their words at me. I kept thinking. There had been no windows. I had no idea whether it was day or night, or how much time had passed that I'd been out. No, wait, it had to be nighttime. There were vampires at those tables and they were awake, so it couldn't be sunlight out...wherever out was.

I did the math. I had been unconscious for at least eight hours. They must have gotten me out of the restaurant before Sam came back, but what had happened to her? If she was here too, she'd have come over or been in the cage with me. She must have gotten away, but with no way to find me.

Why had they taken me, anyways? I hadn't done anything to gain suspicion in the all of ten minutes I'd been in there, except...

Except I had given them Shu's cover name. They *had* known he was a fucking cop. That's why he'd been in the ring. They knew. So when we came looking for him, they knew I was too. Had the guy at the sandwich shop made me first? Or had the girl at the coffee place tipped him off we were coming?

Fuck. Fuck, fuck, fuck.

I hoped Sam had gotten away, at least. If she hadn't and wasn't here... I really didn't like the alternative, so I was going to stay optimistic and believe she was still free. She was a good cop, a smart one, so she had a really good chance for getting away once she knew something was wrong. She could be the cavalry.

I was going to need the cavalry.

Adrenaline began again as my anxiety rose. How was Sam going to have any clue where I was? And how was she going to find out without getting caught herself? Would I survive long enough to give her a chance to find me, or would I end up like Shu?

A stupid plan. A stupid, stupid, *stupid* plan. Why had I agreed to this?

Sadie, oh god, Sadie. I was filled with overwhelming despondency at the idea of ending my life here with things left the way they had been between us. Why hadn't I talked to her before I went to work? It wouldn't have killed me. This had a good chance of doing that, and I'd stormed out on her like a petulant teenager because my feelings were hurt.

I hated myself right then, and everyone around me.

I pressed my eyes into the crook of my elbow and tried to pretend that all of existence no longer existed.

☾O☽

A while later—I don't know how long, might have been minutes or hours, but it felt like forever—someone came up to my cage. This wasn't the same guy who had come up to me earlier. This one said nothing, just unlocked the door and walked away.

I groaned and rolled over, pushing myself to my hands and knees before staggering to my feet. I still felt pretty awful in the head, and everywhere else, but if the cage was open, I damn well wasn't about to stay inside. I pushed open the gate, which creaked loudly, and cautiously made my way out into the general population.

Everyone was a danger to me. Seeing as how we were all prisoners here, I was certain that was unfair and paranoid, but I couldn't help it. I'd already been drugged and abducted from a fucking sandwich shop, so how was I supposed to feel? Besides, they all looked to feel about the same about me, judging from the glances I got as I slowly made my way to an empty seat on one of the benches.

Sitting down, I realized there were plates of food on the table. Everyone had what looked like a pounded tin pie plate, and all I could think about was how this was like some cliché prison movie. I would have laughed if it was at all funny.

What was on the plate in front of me looked like overcooked, greasy ground beef. I didn't eat it and pushed it away. A shifter across from me—I couldn't tell his animal because there were too many other smells—grabbed the plate and ate the food in two mouthfuls. I watched and tried to keep the expression of revulsion off my face.

"It's not very appetizing, is it?" a small voice asked from my right.

I jumped and jerked my head around, seeing a young woman beside me. I hadn't heard her walk up or sit down. She was somewhere in her twenties, I ventured to guess, and small. Shorter than Sadie, who was 5'4", so I guessed this one just over 5' and not a hundred pounds soaking wet. With little feminine figure to speak of, I'd have guessed her an adolescent but for the look of her face and in her eyes. Her expression was a kind one, but there was just something that told me she wasn't a kid.

"No, it's not," I had to agree, because it was true.

"I know it doesn't seem like it, but you will get used to it." She smiled a little, although it was one of those smiles that said, 'it sucks but it will happen.' I noticed when she spoke this second time that she had an accent, although I could only figure as much as Eastern Europe. Not Russian, but maybe not far.

I grunted, because I had a hard time envisioning it, even though I knew she was right from a practical sense. If that was all I'd get to eat, I'd eventually eat it. Today was not going to be that day, however. It had been a bad enough day already.

She was quiet for a while before piping up again, "My name is Lucia Vasile."

"Vance Johnston." I figured what the hell, might as well use my own damn name since I was screwed anyways. "Lucia Vasile," I repeated after a moment. "Not a very common name."

"Not really, no," she said. "I wasn't born in the U.S."

I nodded, having found that likely with her accent. "Where are you from?" I was too hazy to try to guess.

She started drawing invisible and thus indiscernible shapes on the metal table with the tip of her middle finger. "I was born in Romania," she said, "and my family immigrated when I was in my early teens."

She wasn't wholly human. I could tell that much by the fact she was here, but it was also a sense. I couldn't smell psychic abilities the way I could vampires and shifters, but I got this faint tingling at the ends of every sense and I knew she had powers, and they were strong. I didn't know what and it wasn't polite to ask, because I cared about manners right then... I just knew this little creature beside me had a lot of power bubbling inside.

I was staring and didn't realize it until she caught me. "Animator," she answered the question I had been determined not to ask. I raised my brows, and she smiled distantly. "You looked curious, and that seemed the most likely thing for you to be curious about, in this place and all."

"You're very perceptive."

The smile faded, and the distance grew. "I've been here

a while," she said, "so I've seen a few people come through. Things fall into patterns, even when the people change."

Her expression disturbed me on a level I couldn't consciously access to analyze or consider. "I guess people are all the same, in the end."

"No." She shook her head slowly. "People are different, but a single situation can simply prompt the same reactions from people. I believe that's inherent of the situation rather than the people."

My head hurt too bad for philosophy, so I just nodded. "Perhaps you're right."

She nodded as well. "Do you know what you're here for?"

"Bread and circuses," I commented, kind of to myself but I saw both of her brows lift and guessed she didn't get the reference. "I think I'm going to get put into the ring and they'll expect me to tear someone apart." I had left my filter in the cage, apparently.

"Pretty much," she agreed meekly, almost apologetically. I had no idea why she was apologetic, because I was fairly convinced this slip of a girl wasn't the one kidnapping people, imprisoning them, and making them fight. If she was, she was the world's best actress.

CHAPTER NINE

After dinner was finished, as much as you could call it that, one of my fellow prisoners gathered the dishes and carried them to a metal bin in the corner. I thought maybe someone would come collect them and wash them, but then again, judging by the terrible smells in this place, I wasn't going to depend on it. I tried to ignore that corner as best I could while everyone milled around despondently.

"I would have expected more resistance and activity, even in a prison, from a bunch of preternatural beings," I commented to Lucia, who had remained beside me.

"Everyone is, when they first get here," she said ruefully. "But this place has a way of beating you down, literally and figuratively."

I frowned, because I began to understand what she meant. And it wouldn't be long before I understood better.

Metal clanged loudly from the far end, and a gate swung open. Two guards marched in while two remained at the door. They carried weapons and attitude in plentiful supply, but no one gave them any trouble as they grabbed two prisoners. They went without argument, and the gate was shut behind them. Before I had the chance to say anything more to Lucia, a row of television screens encircling the entire 'common area' of our prison came to life.

It was the arena I had seen on the monitor back at the station, which suddenly seemed like a lifetime ago. The guards led the prisoners they'd just removed into the cement crater, one to each side. They left them, and I heard more gates shutting inside the thick cement walls.

The prisoners now in the arena were one man and one woman, though not far apart in size. I hadn't the chance before they were removed to figure out what they were beyond that, and both looked more defeated than anything—people-sized balloons that were slowly losing air.

Inside the arena and our cell, yellow lights began flashing and then remained solid, giving everything an amber tint.

"Yellow means the battle is non-lethal," Lucia answered a question I hadn't asked.

"They don't look like they're going to fight at all," I said, trying to figure out what I was really seeing. The pieces of the puzzle were so incongruous that they didn't really make any sense to me.

My new little friend sighed deeply. "Just watch."

I broke my gaze away from the television screens and looked at her, but she said nothing more as she watched the screen above us.

As I turned back to watch, I saw something happening. There was a mist or a fog slowly filling in between the concrete walls, and I could see no clear indication of where it was coming from. As it did, however, the audience I also couldn't see began roaring their applause. The stands must have been circling the top. The sound was deafening, but what I found more noteworthy was the change that came over the two people as the mist settled upon them. It seemed to drift *into* them, and their utter dejection became bloodlust.

"What just happened?" I asked her.

"I don't really know," she replied. "No one in here does. We just know that no matter how much we *don't* want to fight, once that mist is upon us, we have no choice and become like other people. We don't know ourselves while it is upon us, but the real curse is that we remember it when it's over."

As if I hadn't thought all of this was bad enough already. To watch these captives fighting was terrible, but to watch them controlled by such means and against their will was somehow even more…horrific.

The two launched themselves at one another like animals, bare hands curled like claws as they latched onto each other's skins and raked bloody stripes over each other's hides. The dark-haired woman had a slight size advantage, looking more muscular than the man. She grabbed him by the throat and lifted his feet off the ground, launching him into the cement wall. The sickening crack was a loud one, but as soon as the smaller one hit the floor, he was back on his feet and surging forward. His shoulders collided with her knees and kept with her until they were both in the wall.

With the darker one backed against the cement, the tackler began a furious attack of fists into the woman's midsection. This went on for what seemed like a full minute before she slammed her head forward into the head of the other, sending him reeling back several steps. That was more than enough of an opening, but the dark one roared instead and suddenly her body started shifting.

So, shapeshifters. But it seemed like the worst time to start a shift. It could take almost a minute to do it, and that was sixty vulnerable seconds. Yet there must have been a pheromone with it, because instead of attacking, the other began to shift too.

This fight was about to get a lot bloodier.

Where the larger, darker one had been now stood a sleek, black panther. And where the other one had been now stood a wolf. The wolf was big even for a shifter's animal form, which are always bigger than the animal in nature, and the pair looked evenly matched. I couldn't help but wonder if this had been on purpose, or just a happenstance of who had been grabbed.

The wolf dove, and the panther swiped. Suddenly, they were moving almost too quick to recognize each action. I saw flashing claws and teeth and blurs of fur. And every time the furball paused, there was more flesh hanging open—ragged, raw, and red. Blood was spattered on the floor, with new, bright red dripping against the old, darkened blood of past fights.

Suddenly, there was a pained yelp, and the wolf collapsed. The panther was about to dive in for the kill, but large darts flew in from either side and struck both animals. The panther collapsed on top of the wolf, and people in black came out to carry the heavy bodies out. It was only a few minutes before they were brought into our holding area and tossed in separate cages, like I had been when I first awoke. Then the guards left.

I walked over and knelt by the cage. I felt more than saw Lucia follow me, like a tiny shadow.

"How long will they be out for?"

"It varies," she said with a shrug, kneeling beside me. She looked at the panther with pity before turning that gaze to the wolf. "I have yet to see a pattern according to size, or species, or fatigue, victory or loss. The only thing is that vampires seem to come out a little quicker and psychics a little slower, but it's not an exceptional difference."

I thought about that for a while, although nothing really came to me. "And that aggression will have worn off by then?"

She nodded.

Sighing, I put my hand on the bar. It singed for a moment, but I ignored it. I almost liked the pain. It helped me focus. "This needs to stop."

"It does," she agreed easily, "but I'll be damned if I know how to do it." She paused. "Although I guess we are all already damned."

☾○☽

We sat in silence for a little while, but it felt like it couldn't be more than ten or fifteen minutes before the gate opened again. I jumped, high-strung and not expecting the noise. Another two were dragged out, just like the first. This time, two women. I looked at Lucia, but she seemed unsurprised.

"There are always at least two fights a night," she explained.

The two of us were sitting on the floor and leaning against the wall beside the cage. I didn't want to leave the cat. Probably because she was a cat, which made us kind of kindred. Or maybe I was clutching at straws.

No matter where you sat in this prison, you had a view of the televisions. Unless you wanted to put your head to the floor, but I wasn't keen to give a vulnerable shot to anyone... just in case. Although no one in this place looked like they were on the verge of attacking anyone.

The lights that had been yellow now flashed blue, and the difference was eerie. I turned back to Lucia, who again was kind enough to read my mind. "Special request," she explained. "That means someone with money requested one or both of those fighters especially. They might be in the audience, or they might be watching at home. It's an amazing thing, technology."

I couldn't disagree, and yet I wanted to. Maybe just for the sake of it.

On the screens, I saw fog filling the arena, but I couldn't bear to watch again. I sighed and turned to look at the unconscious animal beside me. Her breathing was even and seemed peaceful. I wish I could do the same. Maybe if I banged my head against the bars hard enough...

I wondered what was going on beyond this place. Was Sam okay? Had she gotten away without being caught? I sincerely hoped so, for her sake and mine. I had to hold onto the hope she had gotten away, because she was my best hope for getting out of here. She was my best hope for help, because otherwise, it would be a while before anyone realized I was missing.

And Sadie… God, I didn't want to think about her, but how could I not?

If Sam had gotten away, then Sadie would know by now I was in trouble. My heart ached to think of what she must be feeling. But, if she knew then Dakota knew, and that woman was grumpier than anyone on the planet, but she was the best damn hunter I had ever met. She had tracked an ancient (a vampire over a thousand years old), and they're damn near impossible to find if they don't want to be found. If anyone on the planet could find me, it would be Dakota.

Still, I couldn't stop hating myself. If I died here, then the last time Sadie would ever have seen me… And if I died, that would be the second love of her life to die on her, and as much as I didn't want to die for lots and lots of very good reasons, I didn't want to do that to her. I couldn't. I wouldn't. I had to live. I had to make it out of here.

"Oh dear," I heard Lucia say quietly.

I looked at her and then at the screens, but no one was on them now. There were steps, and I watched the guards come toward our bars, but instead of opening the gate, they followed the path around it to a corner so shadowed I hadn't much noticed it. They each had a body over their shoulders, and they dropped them into the dark before marching away without a word. I could see the bodies, somewhat. One was bloody and looked like parts were missing. The other seemed in better shape.

"What happened?" I asked, confused.

"It was supposed to be a non-lethal match," she explained. "They all are unless otherwise stated. But one killed the other, so that one was executed for not following the rules."

Worse and worse yet, I thought. "But that mist puts them out of control, so how can they..." I trailed off, stopping myself. Looking for logic from people who kidnapped, imprisoned, and forced people to fight? That seemed like a stupid thing to try to do. "So they just killed her."

Lucia nodded. "Yes. They do that, although they try not to kill too many of us unless we start overcrowding."

Scrubbing my hands over my face and through my hair, I breathed out harshly and tried to think. My brain didn't want to work.

"This just keeps getting better and better."

CHAPTER TEN

No one else came, and there were no other fights that night. Eventually, I had to go to sleep. I didn't want to, but I had little choice when my body decided I would pass out after the stress and the adrenaline of the day and night.

Not that sleep was peaceful. I dreamed, and it was a night full of my subconscious assaulting me. A lot of it revolved around variations of the same idea: the image of me dead and Sadie leaning over my body, sobbing dryly. Vampires don't cry because they have no liquid left in their body—except for the blood that's not gone or that they drink—but they feel, and I saw her wailing the sort of agony that was painful to me in ways I can't even express now. I wish I could properly describe the sound and make you understand it, but the words are beyond me.

It was awful. We'll put it that way. And I saw it over and over again, in different places and with my body dead in different ways, but always that: me dead and her broken. *Broken.*

A few other images came and went in between these, but usually on the same theme of me dying in this place, of me being forced into that arena and then torn apart, my family and friends wailing over different pieces of me. That one was particularly fun, I have to say. My mother and father crying over my head. Sadie with my torso. Nykk and Sam with a leg each. Blood everywhere.

Yeah, that was peachy. I woke up in a cold sweat after

that one. I had no idea what time it was on the outside, and that was disorienting. I kind of swayed against the floor, feeling the cold concrete against my body and feeling like my subconscious had been physically beating me up as well as mentally and emotionally.

Somehow, I did fall back to sleep and woke up a while later, after another cheerful litany of death and decay in my dreams.

When I woke up again, the panther in the cage beside me was stirring as well. I heard the tell-tale cracking of bones and popping of muscles that signified a shifter changing. I didn't watch. Shapeshifters are an unusually immodest bunch, but still, it seemed impolite. When the squishing and snapping had stopped, I looked over to see the woman I'd seen in the arena. She looked tired and hazy. Her eyes were taking a while to focus. She had a soft, pretty face, although her cheeks were slightly sunken from a clear lack of nutrition. I wondered how long she had been here. Her skin was pale.

"Did I kill him?" she asked groggily and then frowned. "No, I'm alive." She turned and looked at the other cage, seeing the wolf still asleep. "At least there's that, I guess." Looking down at herself, she checked over the healing injuries. "Not as bad as last time, at least."

I was trying to figure out if she knew I was there and was talking to me, or if she was just talking to herself. That was answered a few moments later when she looked at me, her eyes focused and dark brows knit. "You're new."

I nodded. "Yes, I am. I'd ask if you're okay, but that seems like a stupid question."

"A little," she agreed.

Lucia appeared as if by magic and passed some clothing through the bars. The panther took it with a small, grateful smile. "You're such a doll," she said and then turned to me again as she carefully got to her feet and started pulling on the just-this-side-of-prison-issue garb. "You've met, I presume."

I nodded. I was about to introduce myself when the gate opened and a guard came in. The man didn't speak to anyone and almost no one looked at him. He unlocked both cages like he wasn't worried at all about someone pulling something, but that proved to be just fine because nobody did. He left the cage doors open and left.

The panther walked out slowly, still in pain and fatigued from the night and the drugs. She made her way to a table and I followed, as did Lucia, and we all sat down. I realized now there was bread and pitchers of water. Literally, bread and water. It wasn't the food so much as the cliché that was insulting, but I ate and drank anyways.

"Vance Johnston," I finally got the chance to introduce myself in between the difficulty of eating bread that tasted like it had gone stale before preternaturals were made legal.

"I thought you looked familiar." I frowned, but she was continuing, "Erica Roderick."

My brows shot up. Her face wasn't familiar, but her name was. "I wasn't working your case, but I remember it. You're that reporter."

She nodded. "That would be me."

Now on top of everything else, I felt like the stupidest detective on the face of the planet to not recognize a face from the news. But like I said, it hadn't been my case.

Erica Roderick, twenty-five, reporter for the Adelheid Chronicle. She had been writing articles on recent criminal activity in Adelheid and surrounding areas, connecting it to other towns, and now I remembered she had made some mentions of Blackwood Family connections...

She had disappeared two months ago, and there had been no leads in almost that long. Blackwood was good.

I was fucked.

I tried to not think like that. "Apparently, you were right," I said, because I knew she knew what I meant. I was betting she'd been thinking about it a lot over the past two months in this hell. Man, she had been alive here for two months. She was good.

"Lucky me," she said with a sigh. "I get the breaking story of my life and think I'm gonna be that star journalist I always wanted to be. Instead, I get kidnapped out of my own damn house and dropped here."

'That sucks' didn't really seem to cut it. "You've survived."

She snorted. "I have at that, although I don't really know why. It's been two months with no sign of escape." After downing a cup of water, she said, "How the hell did they get you, though? You're called one of the best cops in Adelheid. I've called you that myself. So, how did you get stupid enough to get stuck here?"

I looked at her for a long moment. "That's amazing. Ego boost and sucker punch in one shot." Not that she was wrong. "An undercover cop died in that arena, and we got to see it live and in color. We didn't know his cover was blown, so my partner and I went undercover as associates of his. They got me." Should I have been talking about all of this to people I just met and had the pleasure of being imprisoned with? Maybe not, but what the hell? Why not?

"Is your partner here?" she asked.

"No, but I don't know if that means she got away or..." I trailed off, because that statement did not need to be finished. "We were separated, me inside and her outside, when they took me, so she had a chance."

Lucia finally spoke up. "I hope she did." Her voice was small, like a little kid.

I turned to her and tried to smile reassuringly. "I hope she did, too."

"Undercover cop," Erica was saying. "You mean Detective Shu."

That brought me right back around to her. "Yeah. Did you know him?"

She nodded. "Yeah, from in here. He wasn't as undercover as you thought, I'm sorry to say, Detective."

I frowned. I wasn't going to like this. "What do you mean?"

"Shu was dirty," she said plainly. Tact probably wasn't a skill they worked on here, but then, who needed tact? "He worked for the Blackwood Family for years, playing their inside man on the force. Was how they were so slippery for so long. I always suspected they had someone inside but didn't have a hint of proof. But Blackwood turned on him, and that's how he got here. Got pretty chatty behind bars."

"He was working for Blackwood?" I had heard her fine, but I couldn't help but repeat the question dumbly. I didn't want it to be true, so maybe I could convince myself that I had heard wrong.

"For years," she said. Well, there went that.

I covered my face with my hands, feeling even more like the stupidest cop to ever walk the face of the earth. Not only did I get my ass in this position by rushing undercover into a situation where my cover was blown before I got there, but now it was for a dirty cop. I was avenging someone that would've thrown me under the bus...who *had*, in many ways.

Not that I felt anyone (almost anyone) deserved to die the way he did, but it did change things, and it made my situation fall into a different light.

"I'm sorry," Lucia said quietly beside me, and I felt a small hand on my shoulder.

"Thanks." I sighed, dropping my hands again. I looked at Erica. "Why did they turn on him?"

She shook her head. "He didn't know, but I think they just decided it had been long enough. They're smart and evil. It's been a long time, and Shu could be a little arrogant. They probably figured he was gonna screw up soon and let on. Just taking the job as undercover with the people he was in bed with was a little risky. Maybe it just pissed them off." She sounded like both the voice of experience and of apathy.

I guess I could understand it. "I guess we'll never really know, since he's dead and I doubt the family will be talking to me about it."

☾O☽

Time passed. There wasn't much to do between 'meal' times. The televisions stayed dark but for fights. There was nothing of anything in here. No wonder why everyone was going crazy. They just sat around. Except for the vampires. I knew it had to be daylight, at least, because they were a pile of corpses in the corner.

I found myself kind of fading in and out, not quite of consciousness but of a certain level of awareness. Before I knew it, the gate was being opened and something was set just inside the door. I forced my eyes to open and focus, watching a couple prisoners grab the trays and bring them to the table. Getting to my feet, I dragged myself to the table and sat. It was more of the meat-like stuff I didn't know if I could manage to gag that down, but I'd stay sitting. What else was there to do, after all?

"You're a cop?" The voice came from across the table. I looked up from where I'd been examining the slop on my plate.

A woman looked back at me. She smelled human. She had the same worn look that everyone else had, although there was an intensity in her eyes I hadn't seen in anyone else's. Her features were strong, handsome, and she bore into me unblinkingly, and that was a little unnerving.

"Yeah," I said. "I am."

"Dirty?"

I tried to stop my knee-jerk reaction, remembering the last cop that had been in here. "No, but it's the fault of a dirty cop I'm here."

She didn't say anything for a long moment, looking my face up and down like she was evaluating me. I wondered if she was an empath, but I didn't feel the tingles of human magic, so she was probably just reading me like anyone else would.

"Alright." I apparently passed the test. She offered a thin hand across the table. "I'm Elena."

"Vance." I shook it, a little afraid I'd break it if I pressed too hard.

A few moments later, a man sat down beside her. Big guy, probably my height and just about my breadth through the shoulders.

"Daniel," she said, turning to him with familiarity in her gaze and her posture as she leaned toward him. "This is Vance."

Daniel smelled human, too. Dark hair, full beard. I wondered if he'd had that before he got in here or had been in here that long without being able to shave. My exhausted brain started picturing myself after a while, but I stopped the useless thoughts in their tracks.

"Wish I could say it was a pleasure," I said.

He smiled faintly, brown eyes joining the expression, however slight. "How'd you get caught?"

I thought for a moment. "I guess that's probably the first thing you ask people in here, since we all know why we're here."

"Smart guy."

Smart-ass, I thought, but let it pass. "I'm a cop. Got found out. How about you two?"

Daniel was looking at his plate with the same disgust I had been, although I'm betting he'd had a longer time to be doing just that. "I was hired by the family to do some work. Nothing exactly criminal itself, but I knew who they were." He pushed the metal plate away without his hands, and I knew him for a telekinetic. He crossed his arms over his broad chest. "Me and another guy did the magic-technology crossover that is now broadcasting these fights."

I frowned. "It sounds like you did your job. Why are you here, then?"

"Conall doesn't like loose ends."

I thought about that for a moment. Conall, that was the oldest son of the Blackwood Family. "You know him?"

Daniel shook his head. "Not personally, but I knew who I was working for. This whole operation, the fight arena, is his. He's fucking Howard Hughes, though. No one knows what he looks like."

"I'm just a lesson in not dating the wrong guy," Elena chimed in after a long pause between Daniel and I. "Turns out I was dating the younger son. Didn't know about his family till I was in too deep. He was okay, though. So I figured...what the hell? But then his sister hit on me, and I found out he's a right jealous bastard. He blamed me and here I am. In hell." Sighing, she leaned her head on Daniel's shoulder. "Found a better one in here at least."

Love in hell. That was an interesting idea. "What're your powers?"

"Teleporter," she replied despondently.

"Then how are you still in here?" Even a weak teleporter would have been able to get out of this place.

She pointed at the bars of the outer cell. "They're magic. Keeps all of us in here."

"They also drug us," a new voice said from my left. I snapped my head around, suddenly feeling swarmed by new people. No one gave a fuck about me when I got here, but I guessed I was okay now. She smiled a little, but it was more than I'd seen from anyone else, except maybe Lucia. "Chris. Cryokinetic. Wrong place, wrong time. I witnessed them take someone else and got taken with him."

I began thinking I was going to have to start introducing myself that way, so I said, "Vance, weretiger, good cop with really bad luck."

That actually got a faint laugh from across the table.

"What were you saying?" I asked Chris.

"They drug some of the prisoners, if they think the enchantments might not be enough. It keeps the powers suppressed until they're in the ring. The mist gives them their magic back, but then they're knocked out after the fight and drugged again by the time they wake up," she explained.

"The mist is like adrenaline," Elena said. "It overrides everything else in you, until that's all there is."

"The fog bitch," Daniel murmured.

I looked at him. "What is she? Is she a psychic of some sort?"

He started to shrug, until he realized Elena's head was there, so he shook his own instead. "No idea, for sure, but I think she's some kind of fae. I don't know any psychic who can turn themselves into mist and fuck up someone's head that way. Not even a telepath or mind-controller can do it like she does."

Fae would make sense. We knew so little about them, after all.

"Does anyone ever try to escape?" I asked.

"New ones usually try a few times," Chris answered, "until they realize there's no way. The drugs, the enchantments, the guards, this place... It all keeps you locked up pretty good."

"Then the fighting wears down your psyche," Elena said. "Until you stop caring so much."

"There's a chance now," I said, because I had to have hope. I couldn't lose that or else I would be lost too. "I think my partner escaped, and if she did, it's because she knew they took me. She can get help."

The looks on all three faces were the same: suspicion.

"How would they find you? None of us know where we are," Elena said distrustfully.

"My friends," I said with a weak smile. "I've got some of the most talented people in the preternatural races on my side, including the hunter Dakota."

"I read about her in the paper," Chris said, pretty eyes widening as she brushed choppy red hair off her forehead. "She's the best, they say. Caught a vampire over a thousand years old. She tracked that beast in the Appalachian Mountains that no one could find. Is it true she's never failed on a hunt?"

There had been one, I thought, but even that she got in the end. "It's true, and she's a good friend of mine. If my partner got away, she would've gone to Dakota, and she'll be looking for me." I paused, laughing quietly. "If for no other reason than I owe her fifty bucks from our last poker game."

They all smiled a little at that.

"If we do get out of here, the Blackwood Family needs to pay," I went on, a little more seriously. "And I damn well want to make them do it, so I need to know whatever you guys know about them and their business." At their dubious looks, I added, "I'm a cop, and I would make fucking sure no one gets pulled up on charges for anything they've done if you can give me information that will help take them down when we get out of here."

Unless they had lied, I knew none of them were telepaths. But there was still some kind of silent conversation going on between all three that I was not a party to.

"We will," Elena said. I was picking her out as the

decisive one in the bunch. "I don't know I even care if we all go to prison for it. A prison out there will still be a hell of lot better than this place."

No one could disagree with that.

CHAPTER ELEVEN

We spent a while talking, and I probably learned more in that hour or two than the FBI and local cops had learned in the past year or two. Names and places. Stuff I committed to memory, since it wasn't like I could write it down. Elena was the best source on the people, since she had been in the family from a personal angle. Daniel knew the most about the business, since that had been his line in.

Chris didn't have as much to supply, but she offered some information and insight off what the others were saying. Between the three of them, I began to feel like I had a grip on what to do if I ever did get out of here.

When we were done talking, we all drifted to do whatever. I started walking the perimeter of this large cell.

One wall was cement from top to bottom, and the rest were metal bars. You could see beyond the bars, but it didn't mean that helped, because for almost all of the three sides, 'outside' was another cement wall. Our common cage was lined by a cement corridor with one doorway to a staircase as a corner. It was too steep to see up, but light came down.

I forced my brain to work. I can't really remember now what I thought I'd achieve or how long I walked. I tried to think about where I might be, even though I didn't think it would help me get out. Still, I thought it through anyways.

It was mostly a hunch, but I was almost certain I had never left Adelheid. The city was placed where it was for a reason. It had been founded in the eighteen hundreds by

German immigrants, after the Civil War, but preternatural ones. (It had been named for the man's wife.) There was a reason they settled there, and that was because there were magical forces that converged at this point. Some people called them ley lines, but I just knew that freaky shit happened here and had always happened here. The preternatural are drawn to it.

If they wanted to get the most out of the magical imprisonment, then they'd stay in the city. Besides, it was also a focal point for a preternatural audience. And there were risks in transporting the prisoners too far from where they were taken. Keep it simple.

So, I was still in the city. That had to make it easier for Dakota to track me down, if she knew I was missing. All the cement made it feel like a basement, so I was pretty sure we were underground. The cell was underground with the building of the arena on top. That seemed logical, and a good use of space. The Blackwood Family hadn't been around this long and gotten this big by being stupid. They would make the most of what they had.

But what the hell in Adelheid could be housing something like this and managing to do so without anyone knowing?

"Do you really think we'll get out of here?" That little voice belonged to Lucia.

"I don't know," I replied honestly, stopping my pacing and turning to her. "But I have hope."

She smiled sadly. "That's usually the first thing to die in here."

That had been obvious. "I know, but like I said to the others..." Which she had obviously heard. "My partner may have gotten away and if she did, she told the others, and my friends know what they're doing." I paused. "Dakota works for my girlfriend, too. So not only will my friend be trying to find me, but she'll have the..." I paused, feeling my throat catch for a moment. "She'll have the love of my life riding her hard to do it."

Lucia put her hand on my arm. "That's a lot of motivation." She paused. "I'm here alone in this country now. I don't even know anyone knows I'm missing. Anyone that would be worried, at least, and want to find me."

That was just so sad. "How did you get here?" It was apparently the standard question, after all.

Lucia looked away. "I'd rather not say."

Everyone else had been so quick to reveal it that her response surprised me, but I wasn't going to pressure her.

"Look," I said after a long moment. "If anyone can find us, it's Dakota. I can't be sure, but I have hope."

"Alright," she said with a nod.

If she was going to say anything else, she didn't have the chance. The gate opened, and two men in black with big guns walked in. One walked straight for us, and I felt my heart speed up. Holding my breath, I just waited for them to take me. The man was eyeing me, and I didn't blame him. I was too new to be dejected, and I was bigger than him.

But he didn't reach for me. He reached for Lucia.

Out of instinct, I grabbed him and tried to pull him off her. I shoved him into the bars. He cursed and came back at me. I was ready to slug him, but the butt of his rifle got to my chin first. I staggered back a step but was ready for more when I heard Lucia's little voice call, "Vance, don't!"

I stopped and looked at her.

Her dark eyes were panicked. "It's not worth it."

I wanted to argue with her, but I didn't. The guard and I had a standoff for several long, tense moments. He finally hauled her off, along with a young man in the hands of the other guard. The room was watching me, but with what I thought was sympathy in their eyes.

I forced myself to stand still despite the rage I felt flowing through me. The tiger roared, wanting blood. I stared down the guards who came around the corridor, but I couldn't get at them. They were eyeing me, though. Keeping close to the cement wall as they went to the corner where they'd dumped the fighters from the night before. The four guys each grabbed a body from the macabre pile and carried them out.

At first, I was going to ask why, but then I realized Lucia was an animator, so how else was she going to fight?

Forcing myself to breathe now, I stepped back and looked up at the screens. I felt all the blood rush out of me when the room flooded with red light. I knew what that meant.

Someone in that ring was going to die tonight.

It started the same as the others. Lucia and the young man were brought into the arena. They didn't fight it and looked like they would be anywhere but there. I watched them meet gazes across the room in an almost wordless apology. One of them was going to end up killing the other, but there was no malice in those looks. Just sorrow and sympathy.

I felt a moment of existential rage. This was a different fury than what I'd felt before. A few minutes ago, it had been defensive. It had been fueled by my own feelings of impotence. This was about the greater evil. This was about the world I lived in.

The world hadn't been the same after Cameron's Law. Other countries hadn't all followed our lead on that law part, but the whole world knew about us now. They knew vampires and werewolves were real. We weren't just myth and fodder for fiction, but true beings. It was a hard pill to swallow, but much of the country had come to accept us. Hell, several businesses were being smart and marketing to us.

But there was the other side. There was the side that

saw us as monsters, no matter what. They would look at these screens and see us getting what we deserved, and then wouldn't give a damn about the looks in the eyes of those kids. Cause that's all they were. Two kids, couldn't be more than early twenties, who happened to have abilities and be here. And now they were going to be forced to fight to the death.

And there'd be people out there who'd say they deserved it, just for being born different.

That hit me in the gut like a freight train. I'm not sure why I started thinking on that line, but I did, and it just made me feel worse.

I had to get out of here. I had to stop this.

Mist was filling the arena. I didn't want to watch, but I couldn't turn away. I was compelled to keep watching and felt like it would somehow be dishonorable to turn my head and pretend it wasn't happening.

The change took them over as quickly as it had in the other fights, and the sorrow was gone. They wanted to kill each other now, and I watched. Lucia pressed her palms together, and one of the bodies before her rose, followed quickly by the other. Her opponent needed more gestures and I saw his lips moving, but the audio couldn't pick up his words over the noise of the crowd.

Soon, all four corpses were animated, shambling around the arena after the two who brought them back to life and controlled them. As the zombies came for them, they danced away. That was the challenge—not just to avoid the zombies, but to keep control of your own while doing so. I knew from my experience with the animator at the Stanton Agency that it was a bit of magic that took a lot of mental strength and concentration. I saw the effort written on both of their faces as they moved.

The bodies they had been given to raise were relatively new to the land of the corpse, so they had most of themselves intact. That made for a more effective zombie, but even if they had only been dead for a half-hour, nothing could give them back much speed or coordination. They were clumsy things, swaying and stumbling around the ring as they were pushed by magic. Like awkward puppets.

The zombies each scored hits on the animators, but not enough to keep them wrapped up or kill them.

Then something began to change.

One of the zombies stopped and began to turn one way and then the other, like it was twitching or confused. When the male animator's face took on a shade of indignation on top of his bloodlust, I realized what was happening: Lucia was getting control of his zombie. Her magic was evicting his from the spirit of the corpse. It was a fight, as the raised one kept jumping between directives, but eventually, Lucia got it. Now three bodies shambled after one and only one to the other.

One of the three turned and began chasing the other zombie, but this one didn't care it was being pursued. It just kept pursuing its target, since the magic would let it do no less.

I knew who was going to win when the fourth zombie stopped and began twitching like the first one had. The other animator knew it too and came running at Lucia himself. He tackled her and for a moment, the zombies seemed to wander without any direction at all. But only for a moment, before they marched over to the wrestling animators and pulled the man off her.

They threw him to the ground and set upon him. The room filled with the sounds of his screams coming from the televisions and then they stopped. Lucia was on her feet, staring at the remains in her zombie's hands before that dart came out and dropped her.

She was being tossed in a cage for her 'detox' minutes later. I was too disgusted to go for the guards again. So, I went to her cage and knelt beside it, reaching my hand through the bars despite the sizzle and touching her hand.

Chapter Twelve

The gate opened probably fifteen or twenty minutes later. Of course, there was going to be another fight. I ignored the guards this time, focused on my poor unconscious friend as she lay in the cage. She had blood and gore clinging to her dark skin and deep scratches from where the zombies had gotten to her before she wrested control of them.

I knew she was unaware of my presence, but it made me feel better to be there beside her.

But then I was aware of a nearby presence and saw the guards had come for me this time. And apparently recalling the last time they'd been near me, there were two instead of the usual one. I briefly considered fighting, but I didn't. I let them grab me by each arm and haul me out. Where would I go if I did fight them, after all?

As I moved past, I saw another guard grabbing the arm of another man, dragging both of us out of the cell and up the cement steps. There was light above me, which I was now walking into. I felt a strong flash of relief when I saw yellow fill the air and knew I wasn't about to be killed or have to kill someone. Hopefully.

We were dragged into the cement arena I had only seen on monitors until now. It was larger than it had seemed from television, and I couldn't see the audience from in here. But I could hear them, and the sound was deafening.

After the guards had left us and the gates had shut, we were left facing each other.

He looked to be right about my size in both height and breadth, although a little skinnier. He had probably been here a while. His skin was pale, and he had blonde hair and blue eyes. He had a scraggly beard and the same dejected look in his eyes.

"I'm sorry," I said, speaking loud enough to be heard over the crowd.

"Me too."

I inhaled deeply and caught a familiar scent of tiger. Oh, this would be interesting.

"I'm Ivan."

Weakly, I returned a smile. "Vance."

The fog began rolling in, and I sighed heavily. I considered trying to hold my breath, wondering if I'd be spared if I passed out and couldn't inhale again before I was unconscious, but then I realized it wouldn't matter. It sunk into me beyond my skin, being absorbed like humidity. First it was cold, and then I became hot. Hotter than I had ever before felt, like every ounce of my body was about to melt. Then the rage came, like a tidal wave. It started with the feeling of wanting to pull every muscle of mine apart from the agony of it, but then it quickly changed to me wanting to pull every muscle of *his* apart.

It's hard to remember everything now, so hazy as it all was. I was a passenger in my own body, and yet I wasn't. What it felt, I felt. I was enraged, not watching someone else be enraged.

The same look was fully in his cold eyes, and I smiled.

We lunged for each other and crashed with all the grace of two boulders, bouncing off one another and sliding back a step. We caught our balance, and I was the first to recover. I grabbed the front of his dirty, ragged shirt and hauled him off his feet, tossing him into one of the walls. The thud was audible, and I enjoyed the sound. He rebounded quickly and again we came for one another, undaunted by pain or caution.

Reminiscent of the tigers in our blood, we began taking swipes at each other, wild haymakers raining with all of our supernatural strength. Our fists connected with each other's faces, with no care for protecting ourselves. Small cracks in flesh and bone for us both, and I felt the blood run down from these wounds. It rushed over my lip, and I tasted the blood.

I liked it.

With the guy getting in close, I was able to grab his head in both hands and drive it down into my knee. Something cracked and he screamed, but he didn't waste time with the pain as he drove his fists up into my body. First into my torso, and I felt the breath being pushed from my lungs. As one hit spun me around, his fist caught me in the lower back—kidney shot—before that turned me and he caught me in the throat.

I coughed and retched. I didn't care for the pain, but my body was aware of a sudden lack of breath and responded instinctively. He came for me again, but I was at least able to slide and jump back away from his hits. I tried to growl, but the sound came out raggedly through my damaged throat.

Finally, I had gasped in enough air to get beyond the injury and surged back into him. We traded more hits to the face and body, sometimes the human in us used our fists while the cat in us caught the other with open palm, claws-out swipes. Blood was flowing freely from both of us now, bruises and welts already rising ugly.

Again, we came at each other in a great collision of flesh, but this time, the force was so much that we ended up on the floor. I had fallen backward and had Ivan atop me, where he tried to get at my face. I was able to catch both of his wrists with my hands and yank his arms to either side. My strength and reach were greater, and I heard a popping noise from his shoulder.

He reared back with a roar of pain, and I threw him off. Landing on the shoulder I had just injured, now it was a scream, and I enjoyed the sound. Scrambling up, I tackled him where he lay and again went for the bad shoulder before grabbing his hair and slamming his head into the concrete floor. He flailed against me, but only one arm had any power to it, and I was in the position of strength.

I kept slamming until his fight slowed and stopped.

Then I felt a tell-tale sting on the back of my neck, and I roared with anger as my subconscious understood what that meant. My last thought before falling unconscious was that I was sad I hadn't killed him.

❰O❱

I think it was the next day by the time I finally woke up again.

If you thought maybe I woke up feeling guilt first, I hate to say it, but I didn't. That came later. I just felt…numb. The realization of what I had nearly done came to me when I looked at the blood on my hands and felt it on my face, but it was worse yet for what I had wanted to do. Having the experience explained to you couldn't compare with the reality of it.

Scrubbing at my face, trying to get the dried blood off, I knew at least that my body had healed or was healing many of the injuries already. That didn't mean I wasn't sore as fuck, but at least I wasn't still so damaged.

But I was distracted by the sound of sobbing just outside the cage. I forced myself to get up and turn toward the sound, finding the small body of Lucia clinging to the bars. I didn't hear the same sizzle sound, because human psychics are still more human than preternatural and such enchantments won't hurt them as much.

"Lucia?" I asked dimly, still not entirely in the world of the coherent.

"I killed him," she hiccupped between her quiet sobs.

Right. The fight from the night before came to me, and I made myself sit up, moving closer to her so I could put my hands on hers. "You couldn't help it," I said, talking as much to myself as to her with that one.

My words didn't seem to help her any better than it helped me, although maybe being a cop helped me a little to not be crying. Or maybe it was because I hadn't killed my opponent, even if the bloodlust had wanted me to.

She sobbed harder. "He was my friend," she wailed softly.

I leaned my head against her fingers in a rather cat-like gesture of comfort, but it was an innate drive for me. I didn't even think about it until after I had already done it.

"I'm sorry, Lucia," I said quietly, because I really didn't know what else to say.

"We're not dis..." Her words disappeared in another torrent of tears and incoherent sorrow.

I nuzzled her knuckles.

Taking a moment and a shuddering breath, she began again, "We're not disposable people." Her voice was a whisper and just so...fucking sad. "Why do they treat us like this? What did we ever do to them?"

I couldn't answer her, because I knew her question stretched beyond this cell. And I had no answers to give.

☾O☽

Eventually, she quieted down, and the guards came to let us out. I couldn't help but notice the guards were looking at me a lot more warily than they had before. In fact, I was the only prisoner they seemed to notice now.

If only I had paid more attention to that, I may have seen it coming.

Chapter Thirteen

Lucia brought me some clothes, and I joined everyone at the table for our 'meal' of whatever it was. I noticed I had apparently developed a little following. Once I sat down, I was joined by not only Lucia and Erica, but Elena, Daniel, and Chris. No one talked about the fights. No one looked at Lucia sidelong for what had happened or commented about my fight.

Ivan seemed to avoid me, but I could hardly blame him. I wouldn't want to hang around me either.

My new friends, however, were very nice. Even though they didn't talk to me about the fight, I could see understanding and sympathy in their eyes.

"Tell us about your girl on the outside," Chris said with a small smile. I had mentioned Sadie, of course, although I hadn't talked about her much.

"She's…" I trailed off, trying to think about how to describe her. "She's a vampire, first off."

There was a quiet laugh from everyone. "Vampires and shifters don't always get along so well," Elena commented.

That made me smile. "We didn't, at our first meeting," I agreed. "I grew up with the usual shifter uncertainty about vampires and still felt it after the law and all. She came in to report being attacked. I guess I was a smart-ass, but so was she." My smile grew. I knew it but couldn't stop it. "I was kinda fascinated by her, I guess. She didn't take any crap from me, and I liked that. We ended up working on a case together, and I… I don't really believe in love at first sight, but I know I fell fast.

"Been together about two years now. I mean, you're all preter, so undoubtedly you've heard about Sadie Stanton."

"I've written about her," Erica said knowingly.

Everyone had a similar knowing look. My girl had, after all, been something of a poster child for preternatural rights. Her and her then-boyfriend (prior to his death) had been the first to come forward, and they championed our cause. I had known of her then, as much as anyone, but still had no idea of how much drive she had, such strength.

"We didn't part well before I left for this assignment," I admitted after a few moments. "In fact, we had a huge fight and I stormed out. I didn't talk to her before I left, and now I'm here."

"But we may get out yet," Chris said, trying to sound optimistic, even if there was uncertainty in her gaze as well.

"I hope so," I agreed.

The rest of the day passed. We sat and talked, or just tried not to think. By the time evening came, I just waited for the gate to open. I wondered who was going to be taken next, but then I saw three guards come in. They all stared right at…

"Me?" I frowned.

"They never take someone two nights in a row," Daniel said, also frowning.

I hoped I was wrong, but I wasn't. The two came for me, and I couldn't help but glare at them. They didn't look scared, as they had the guns after all, but they were still wary as they dragged me out.

Ahead of me, they were pulling a woman.

"Shit," I heard Elena say.

"Ariel is a monster." That was from Lucia.

I didn't know the woman ahead of me, but I smelled the lingering scent of the grave on her and knew her for a vampire. The words and horror of the others didn't make me feel any better about things, and I still couldn't help but wonder why they were taking me again.

As we ascended the stairs, red flashed ahead, and my horror was complete. I pulled against the guards, but they had me firm and I threw me into the arena before I could summon the strength to stop them.

This Ariel and I turned to one another. She didn't look as depressed as the others, but she didn't look eager either. Her hair was red, and I couldn't help but think of the movie, although she was wearing more than a seashell bra. Her eyes were dark. I put her a couple of inches taller than my own vampire, so that made her about 5'6" or 5'7".

"I don't want to kill you," she said. "I'm sorry that I'll have to."

"I don't want you to kill me either."

She smiled a little, though there was clearly no joy in that look.

"How are you so sure I'll be dying?" I had to ask.

Ariel shrugged. "Eleven red-light matches."

She was still here, so that was pretty telling. My heart slowly slid from its usual spot in my chest down through my stomach and somewhere into the bottom of my feet, staring my mortality almost literally in the face.

If I'd been given any more time, I probably would have cracked from the idea, after two days without real sleep, no food, and one fight down already. I didn't get that time, however, because the fog rolled down from the audience I couldn't see. I almost welcomed the fury it would bring, because then I wouldn't be afraid.

You're probably thinking I would be saying I wasn't freaking right the fuck out, that I was facing my imminent death bravely. That my courage was fitting my being a preternatural and a cop. You know what? I could say that, but it would be pure and utter *bullshit*. I didn't want to die. It was plain and simple as that. I did not want to die, and I certainly didn't want to die in that damned, cold arena. Alone. With Sadie thinking that I...

No. I didn't want to die, and I was fucking terrified.

But the ice seeped in and sunk fast through my body, and the fire was right behind it. The rage flowed.

It was the time for blood.

No actual thought was required, because I was intimately familiar with the way the average vampire thinks and acts. It was hard-wired into me, so I was ready for her when the first thing she did was leap at me. Fast, almost flying, as both feet left the ground and she came for me with her mouth open, fangs out, claws ready.

But so was I. At 6'1", she had to aim high to get where she wanted me, and that was my throat. I hunkered down, turned my two hands into one solid fist, and swung at an upward angle. I caught her, mid-leap, with my big hands at the throat and jaw. The force of the swing sent her flying all the way across the arena, hitting the wall. The cat in me took over and I lowered myself, the predator ready to strike again. She was on her hands and knees, licking a split down the corner of her lips, as she stared at me.

She smiled, like she was impressed, before she began a fast spider-like crawl toward me. It would have been slow for a human to do that, but vampires aren't what they used to be. She was fast and almost on me before I knew it, but hunching down like I was, I lunged forward and we met, hard. I went for her head with short, forceful shots. I wanted her down. She swiped at me, trying to get at my mid-section and use those sharp fingernails to drop my guts on the ground. My arms were longer and my knuckles snapped into her, driving her head back.

My shirt was shredded, but I was rejoicing in the music of my fists connecting with her, right up until the moment she ducked my swings. I growled when I felt those claws swipe across the back of my thigh. Ham-strung, my knees bent and lowered my center of gravity. I tried to keep myself from ending up on my ass and at her mercy, when I felt her leap on my back.

Her fingers drove into the muscles of my shoulders, holding hard as she prepared to sink her teeth into my neck and shred me. Vampires were all the same, but I wasn't going to let her. Reaching back, I got a hold of her by the hair and head. She let out an indignant shriek as I forcibly hauled her over my shoulders, feeling the skin her claws had been in tearing as I did so. I flung her toward the floor. Her ear tore off in my hands and made it slippery. She flew farther than I wanted, but I still got her on the ground.

Her red-haired head was right there. Face up. I wasted no time in driving down with my knee, having every desire to crush her skull.

She saw me coming, and I saw the alarm and fury in her eyes as her hands drove into the cement, nails breaking instantly but giving her enough traction to slide away and let my knee hit concrete.

Looking up, I saw she was already on her feet, but facing the wall. I launched myself forward, racing on all fours. The tiger inside was busting free, nearly tearing out of my skin, although I kept it from taking over. I wouldn't let the bitch have my neck while I was shifting, but the tiger wanted in on this. I ran at her as she ran the wall, using its curvature to draw her around. I followed, hot on her heels despite the speed of the vampire being with her.

I smelled her blood on the air, on my hands as I left prints in it across the floor. It filled my nose and almost blinded me. Maybe it would have, if I wasn't so focused on getting to her. The prey was on the run, but she wasn't fucking getting away. I wanted to taste that flesh between my fangs, which I felt pressing into my gums and lips. The tiger was sprouting across my face, making the arena and the prey even more pronounced than before.

Coming to a halt, she was already pivoting on her heel with her arm out, ready to tear me apart with what claws she hadn't left in the cement behind us. In the split-second I saw her move, I bounded off the floor and hit the wall. The tiger's speed drove me on, and I rebounded off the wall and right around her. I hit the ground behind her and forced her to spin again. I relished the look of shock on her face as I leaped up, coming from below and catching her right in the throat.

With fangs and teeth firmly attached, I drove her smaller body to the ground with all the weight I possessed. She thrashed against me, teeth snapping and claws grappling at me, but I had her. Her angry shrieks slowly drowned out in gurgling as old blood bubbled up from the wounds I delivered. Hands and mouth, I ripped pieces of her from her body and swallowed bits of meat. I didn't care about the taste so much as the frenzied act.

A voice was shouting into the arena, but I didn't understand what was said. Then something happened I had never seen: the fog came back out of me. As it did, I was aware of it rising to the stands, and I was myself again.

I threw myself off the mangled body below me and scrambled back to the wall, staring in abject horror. I had seen what I'd been doing but hadn't cared. Now, I cared. I tasted dead flesh and blood, folded myself in half, and began vomiting.

While I was in the midst of coughing up pieces of a vampire, hands grabbed me and dragged me from the arena. I kept hacking and gagging as they did, not even thinking of what was going on.

I was dropped in the cement corridor outside the cell, although I was not brought into the cell itself. From a door behind me I had never even noticed, a tall, broad man came walking up as I sat on my knees. I had managed to stop retching, if barely. I looked up to see a distantly familiar face, a cold, cruel one. He smelled like a vampire.

"You, Detective Johnston," he said in a light Scottish accent, "are a problem for me." He smiled and shook a hand at me. "You talk too much and you know too much, and Ariel should have been it for you."

"You wanted me to die," I said plainly. It was pretty obvious, really. "Didn't you, Conall?" It was a guess, but I was pretty sure I was right. And I had nothing to lose anymore, or so I felt then.

He laughed, kneeling in front of me while the guards held my arms back. "And you are too smart for your own good." He reached behind him and pulled out a gun, which he held to the crown of my head.

I heard my new friends in the cell. Some shouted, while others gasped or screamed.

"Vance!" I heard Lucia call.

"Don't!" That sounded like Elena. And I knew Daniel was at work with the slight quiver of the weapon, but the drugs were too much.

Conall ignored them and held it steady. "Good night, Detective."

He pulled the trigger.

CHAPTER FOURTEEN

Right now, I'm sure you're wondering how I'm telling you this story if I was shot in the head. That's a very good question and not one I actually know the answer to. At least, I don't know why a bullet in my brain didn't kill me instantly. I didn't die the moment it happened. In fact, I was dimly aware of things to follow. Maybe Conall was a really lousy shot, or what happened threw him off. Or maybe I had some telekinetic or even cryokinetic aid. No one could say. And like I said, *dimly* aware, and that doesn't mean time means much to my memories.

The shot was fired, and then there was darkness. A long stretch of black before I began to hear and see things again. Something metal fell down the stairs and then there was an explosion. A smell flooded my sinuses.

I think I was in pain, but then my brain had been pierced. I don't know what I felt.

Shouting and screaming followed the smell. I heard familiar voices and familiar shouts. I heard words I didn't really recognize then, but on reflection (and knowing what I knew later, of course) I recognized "Adelheid PD" and "FBI" in the beloved authoritative shouts.

I think I also heard cries from the other side of my prone body, like "thank you god" and then just "thank you, thank you, thank you." There were wails of gratitude amongst this perception of chaos I had.

Then I felt a presence right close to me. A hand on my

head. Someone said my name. A woman. Sam. "Oh god, no."

"Is he dead?"

"No. But it can't be long."

The chaos diminished, and I was aware of another presence. This one was different, more familiar. My body responded to it before my sluggish brain could, because not just my mind but my *body* remembered.

I couldn't see. Darkness was still around me, but I sensed and heard.

"Vance? Vance! *Vance!*" Hands all over me. Sobbing.

"Sadie, I think…"

"*SHUT UP!*" Her voice was louder in that moment than any human would be able to achieve. It reached down deep and grabbed my heart—my still-beating heart—as it slowed, and I felt the silence closing in on me.

"I won't let him die."

The voice was distant from me, like she was far away now although I still felt her.

Something sharp was at my neck. Feeling was dimming, but I knew something had happened. Then the sensation of more of me draining away just as something was pressed to my mouth. My body reacted to it just as the silence closed in.

☾O☽

Everything came in and out. Lights and dim shapes. Shadows closing in on me.

Sounds I couldn't distinguish. Pain. The sensation of losing everything that was within me. Drifting away, coming back, away and back. The world was nothing but a haze of being, which I could barely touch upon. I recognized little around me.

I was somehow aware that time was passing, but I had no idea how much. I wasn't really thinking. I'm relating this to you now from what I remember, when I look back, but these weren't conscious thoughts I had at the time.

Eventually, though, I truly *woke up*.

The world around me felt dramatically altered. Everything was different. It was brighter, and it was louder. I opened my eyes just to squeeze them shut again, because it hurt like hell. If only I could have closed my ears.

"You'll get used to that."

The voice.

Sadie.

I managed to open one eye enough to look at her. She was sitting in the corner of the room. I recognized it as her bedroom in her house. I was on the bed, but she was sitting on the floor. Her knees were pulled to her chest with her arms wrapped around them, like she was a little kid.

In fact, I realized that she looked...terrified.

"What's going on?" My voice was slurred.

Even as I asked the question, what happened last—that I could know for sure—rushed back. My hands jumped to my forehead. There was no bullet hole, and my whole face was clean of the blood that had been there. Memories of killing that vampire came rushing in next and I felt an urge to vomit, but nothing happened.

I don't know what made me realize it when I hadn't before, but I suddenly noticed that my heart wasn't pounding. In fact, it wasn't beating at all.

Now I forced both eyes open and looked at Sadie. She still looked terrified, but now I had an idea of why. The thought was slow to trickle through my mind as I ran my hands over my body and recollected myself. I was naked, but that obviously wasn't an issue around her. There was a blanket over me, though. I was clean. She must have washed me while I was out. While I was...turning.

Fuck. I was a vampire.

Questions were pouring down on me like rain, but something else was more important. I pushed myself carefully to a seat, but I realized I felt okay. The wounds and fatigue were gone, so I tossed back the blanket and crossed the room with speed that surprised even me.

I pulled Sadie into my arms and kissed her like it was the last thing I would ever do, because it wasn't as far from the truth as I'd have preferred. I held her tight against me, pouring out every emotion I had felt and every thought I'd had since the last time I had been in her house. I slid my hands along her face, holding her head as I all but mauled her. But hey, I think I was allowed.

She seemed so surprised at first that she didn't kiss me back, but it was only a few moments before she poured herself into me. Hands were everywhere, and lips were everywhere. It was just desperation.

Finally, we stopped. I leaned my forehead against hers and breathed her in deep.

"You were dying," she whispered. I opened my eyes but saw hers were still closed. "I was with the cops. They made me wait till the room was safe and Sam had already found you. You were almost dead. Cold was already in you. Vampires know death, you know?" She stopped and gasped softly.

"You saved me." She didn't have to tell me for me to know it was true.

Now, her eyes opened. "How could I not?" she asked. "Vance, I..." She stopped, and her face crumbled. No tears, because vampire, but it was the same effect. "I didn't save Cameron," she said, her voice barely audible. "I wasn't going to lose you too."

I grabbed both of her hands in mine and was bringing

them up to my lips when I felt something. Pausing, I looked at her left hand and saw a ring—a ring that was very familiar—sitting on her left ring finger. Something that had been in a box I had tossed into the yard just beyond the doors I now sat behind…

She caught me looking. "Madison found it when she came home that night," she explained softly. "I've been wearing it since."

I kissed the ring and then pressed my head to her hands. "Will you spend forever with me?" I whispered.

Pressing her cheek to my head, she replied, "Of course I will. And now, we'll have *forever*."

☾○☽

We moved to the bed. I knew there was more to cover, but I just had to hold her for a while to feel like everything was real. Eventually, she got me some blood, and I had to learn to drink it. The physical act was fine, of course, but the psychology of it was a little harder. At least, before I actually did it. Then it was fine.

Fortunately, dating Sadie for two years meant I knew a lot about vampires, so I didn't need the primer. Most of what was left I'd have to learn by experience.

"Sadie," I asked as we sat on the edge of the bed after I'd fed. A thought occurred to me, and I had to ask. "Am I still going to be able to shift?"

"I don't know," she admitted. She bit her bottom lip. "It's forbidden by coven law to turn a preternatural." She hurried to add, seeing my concerned look, "I'm not coven and Jade likes me, so I won't get in trouble, especially given the circumstances." With a weak smile, she went on. "But as such, I don't know."

Getting up, I decided there was no time like the present.

I closed my eyes and urged the shift, but nothing happened. I felt a surge of panic burst in my head, but I told myself to calm the fuck down. I inhaled slowly and forced myself to try again, and after a few tense moments, I felt the tell-tale snap and crack.

A minute later, a relieved tiger was rubbing his fuzzy cheek against Sadie's knee.

I shifted back and got dressed. I was myself again, as much as I could be. It was time to get back to work, and I needed to ask the other questions I had yet to ask and Sadie had yet to answer.

"What happened?"

She knew what I meant without my having to explain further. "Sam saw what happened through the sandwich shop window," she began right off. "At least, right at the end of things. There was no time to get in to help you, and she knew she was next, so she returned to the station to alert people to what happened. Jackson and Kai were right on it, and Jackson called the office. They came and told me, and Dakota took off after you. The cops didn't argue."

"Thank god for Dakota," I said with a half-smile.

She laughed weakly. "A sentence someone never thinks they'll say."

That was hard to disagree with.

"Dakota and the FBI and Adelheid PD were all over it. Dakota was the one to make the trace. They went in guns blazing and got everyone but..." She sighed. "...the one who shot you. The guards that were arrested said he was a Blackwood, but he escaped."

"What about the prisoners?" I asked, thinking of the people I'd befriended.

"Many of them were released, and others are being held."

My temper flared in a way it never had before. "What?!"

I shouted, and she winced at my unexpected volume. I reeled myself back in. "Those people helped me in there."

She looked uncertain, unused to this sort of reaction from me. "Only those that were involved with the Blackwood Family's criminal operations are being held while investigated."

"Damn it!" I slammed my hand against the nightstand, and my fist went right through it with strength I hadn't had before. I grimaced, pulling it free of splintered wood. "I promised them all they wouldn't be arrested if they helped me, and they gave me a ton of information that could get them killed if we don't take Blackwood down. I won't break my fucking promise to them! I don't care if they were guilty in the past. Don't you think they've fucking paid enough after that hell?"

"Vance," she said soothingly, getting to her feet and putting her small hands against my chest. "We'll go to the police station. They want to talk to you anyways, so we'll go and you can talk to them about your friends. It'll be all right."

"Alright," I said, forcing myself to take a deep breath.

CHAPTER FIFTEEN

Not wanting my friends to stay behind bars any longer than they had to, we headed to the station immediately. I was out of the car before Sadie had even put it into park, charging into the building. The officer at the front desk started to speak to me, but I didn't give him time before I was in the squad room.

Sam saw me and was instantly on her feet. I came up short when I saw a nicely pronounced black eye. Blinking, I gestured at it.

She glanced down sheepishly and waved a hand. "Long story," she said, bringing her eyes back up. "I'm glad you're alive."

"Such as it is," I said with a rueful look. "Sadie told me you're holding some of my fellow prisoners here in a cell." I sensed Sadie come up behind me.

"Well, yes," she said, "because they were associated with the criminal enterprises."

I shook my head vehemently before she was even done. "Fuck that. Let them out."

She frowned. Roy came up behind her. "It's good to see you, Detective," he said with a nod to me and Sadie. "Why do we have to let them out?"

"Look…" I tried to keep myself reined in. "I was in hell. Not only were they kind to me, but they helped me. They gave me a ton of information about the Blackwood Family, and they've all been imprisoned. I promised I would help them if they helped me, and they did. We can use their information to catch these sick fucks."

"Tell us what they told you and if the information is good, then they'll be released," Roy promised me after a long moment of thought.

"They've been behind bars for all this time already," I said, almost pleading. I felt Sadie's hand on my back. "This must be horrific for them now."

The captain spread his hands. "Vance, I can't give them anything if I'm not sure they've actually given me something."

I opened my mouth to retort, but the pressure of Sadie's hand got me to stop. "Can I see them?"

He nodded.

Thanking him and nodding to Sam, I left the squad room to head to our lock-up area, where we held people temporarily before they were either released or transferred. I saw my familiar faces, except Chris. She was probably released, but I also saw...

"Lucia?"

She looked up from where she sat, looking embarrassed. "My only family here was my parents," she just started confessing. "They're dead. I had no one. Then I had an opportunity to do some animating work and..." She trailed off. "I never did anything really bad, except be around them at all."

I knelt down beside her where she sat on a metal bench next to the bars. I pressed my hand over hers where it gripped the rod.

"It's okay," I said quietly and then stood back up. "I'm gonna get you guys out of here. I just have to tell folks here what you all told me so my boss knows the information is good, and then he'll let you out."

"Thank you," Daniel said from the corner where he

rested with Elena's thin frame folded against his side. "This is still better than where we were."

❨○❩

Jackson and Kai seemed to materialize at the station as I came back from the holding cell. I was immediately ushered into Roy's office. The five of us—me, Roy, Sam, Jackson, and Kai, as Sadie decided to talk to my new friends while we did 'cop stuff'—made for a rather tight fit, but the new vampire got pity and a chair while the others, excepting Roy since it was his office, had to stand. I didn't really feel bad, I'll admit.

"I'm glad to see you up and about," Jackson said before we dived into business. "You looked like a goner when we came down those stairs."

I was about to ask, "You were there?" But then I realized it was a joint op with the FBI. Of course he'd been there. Especially since he was the one who'd sent me into that trap in the first place.

Roy had already said he was happy to see me, so he moved right on. "What can you tell us?"

Taking a slow breath to collect my thoughts, I started with something I knew they'd want to know. "Shu was fuckin' dirty." That really got their attention as serious frowns passed around the room. "He'd been in Blackwood's pocket for years and ended up in that arena when they turned on him."

"Well, that explains a few things," Sam muttered. "The year of the rat just got longer?"

"And why Shu was screaming in the arena that he didn't belong there," Jackson added.

"He wanted the assignment because he was already in," I went on. "But he had no idea they were about to turn on him."

Kai was next. "Why did they?"

I shrugged. "No one knew, but it was suggested it's just the way they operate. If someone is in too long, they become a liability. They also might have been angry at his taking the undercover job, thinking it was a risk."

"So we sent you into a trap," Roy said.

"Pretty much," I replied. "But we didn't know. We were only able to work off the information we had."

He accepted that with a nod. "What else did you find out?"

"Especially about the Blackwood Family," Jackson chimed in. After all, the interest of the FBI did revolve around that.

"Alastair apparently has almost nothing to do with the business operations anymore," I immediately got into the next part. "He's given that all to the kids, although kids at some-odd hundred years…" I trailed off. "Anyways, so, finding him is going to be hard because his hands are no longer in anything."

"But the kids are, and that's a good start."

"The kids run it all," I went on. "They don't trust any of their underlings to actually control any arm of the criminal operations. They oversee everything at that level and apparently, they're all control freaks.

"Niall is the middle child and the loose cannon. His area is the drug trade and the extortion. He's apparently very selective on the first, though, and they only deal in specific classes of magical drugs. Rumor had it there's a new heroin about to hit the streets laced with a rare herb found in the fae realm."

Kai made a strange noise behind me, but I ignored her. For now.

"But Kenna would have been the one to give the order to kill our two small-time guys a few nights ago." Had it really only been so short a time? It felt like it had been forever. "Kenna is the youngest and only daughter. She's apparently the one who manages the human trafficking and the weapons running. I'll tell you, these guys put every human mafia to shame. Apparently, Niall and Kenna work together a lot, although they fight viciously just as much."

"What about Conall?" Sam asked.

My entire being sunk into shadows as the image of him entered my mind, pulling the trigger. "He's the recluse. His only area seems to be the fighting arena, because he's pulled rank and doesn't want to do the work of the other jobs. And it makes the steadiest money, between the audience paying, the people who hook into the live feed, and the special request fights. No one I talked to had ever seen him before, until he decided to off me." I looked at my hands, trying to contain the rage growing again inside me. "They put me in the arena in a fight they were sure I would lose, because I was talking to the others too much. When I didn't die, Conall took it on himself. Apparently, he wanted a better show of it but figured that death was death."

I felt Sam's hand on my shoulder. I sighed, closing my eyes, but the images got stronger when I did that, so I opened them again. "There was something about him…" I trailed off, frowning.

"Can you describe him?" Kai asked.

So I did. I focused on a blank spot on Roy's desk and dug through the cobwebs that had taken up in my head after all the trauma, pulling out an image of his face as he stared down at me. I described him as best I could, from the shape of his face and coloring to an odd scar across his cheekbone. That had to be an artifact from before he was turned.

Sam was frowning. "That sounds really familiar."

"I thought he looked familiar," I agreed, "but I couldn't place him."

Looking like a woman about to hunt something down, her eyes were already searching while she shook her head in thought and left the office. Those left behind exchanged a look that asked the question, but all came to the same idea that we didn't know what she was thinking. We just had to wait.

She came back into the office a couple of minutes later with a file folder in hand, which she set on Roy's desk. Opening it, she pulled out a photo and showed it to me. "Is this Conall Blackwood?"

I was shocked. "Yeah, it is," I said. "How do we have a picture of him if he's such a recluse?"

Sam smirked. "Because he's a smart fucker who has been hiding in plain sight," she declared. "This is McGrath, the bastard that electrocuted our people."

There was a communal gasp as I ripped the picture out of her hand. "How is that even possible?" I asked. "How did I not remember him? How has he done that? Why didn't anyone know he was a vampire when we have a damned file on him?!"

The winces on the faces of the others told me I'd been losing control of my vampire vocal volume, so I murmured an apology and looked at the image again. "But that's him."

"He was a known electrokinetic, so no one ever thought about him being anything else," Sam said. "And we actually don't have all that much on him. It's more that we just know about him. And who would guess the mid-level Blackwood lieutenant was actually the crown prince?"

"Bloody brilliant," Jackson agreed. "But how…"

"Sadie told me that it's considered, like," I paused, trying to think of the word, "taboo to change another preternatural into a vampire." I didn't mention I got to be Mr. Special Circumstances. They could all guess. "But I can still shift into a tiger, so that means that when they do—at least sometimes—the original powers are kept. Conall was a psychic before his dad turned him."

"This is all fascinating," Roy jumped in, "but the important question is, how do we find them?"

At least somebody in the room was still being a cop and not focusing on paranormal systems. "Right," I said, feeling a little embarrassed. "They were able to tell me some businesses in and around Adelheid that the Blackwood Family operates out of and even occasionally live at. They don't keep any permanent homes, which is part of why they're so slippery."

I gave them the list of businesses, and they all set to finding addresses. Sam was back in the McGrath file, looking to see if there were any known locations or suspected ones in there so that maybe we could compare the two and find some commonalities.

"One thing to remember," I was saying after we'd moved back into the squad room to get more working space. "As I've been told, it wasn't that far from sunrise when y'all stormed the gates. That means that once Conall escaped, he would have to go to ground before it came up. Being older, he could push it some, but I doubt he'd want to press his luck." I pulled up a map on my computer, pinpointing the warehouse I learned the arena had been in.

Sam thought for a moment. "Given the amount of time he'd have between the time he got away from us and sunrise, he could only have gotten this far." She drew a circle with her finger on my screen.

Jackson and Kai came over. "Here's some of the business addresses," he said, and Sam and he leaned in and began pointing to places on the map. I didn't know if they realized how much they were crowding me, and it bothered the hell out of me. More than it would have in the past, I think, but I kept it to myself.

"Only these two are in our radius," Sam said. "So unless

he went somewhere new, I'm betting that he went to one of these." She blew out a breath. "And we just hope he's chosen to lay low for the day."

"Two teams," Jackson said. "We move on them simultaneously and immediately. PD can take this one, while we can take the other."

"You better not be thinking of leaving me behind," I stated plainly, inhaling with relief when they backed up.

They looked like they were going to argue and say I needed more rest or some shit like that, but I guess the look on my face was enough to prevent it.

CHAPTER SIXTEEN

Our strike teams mobilized with amazing rapidity. Maybe it was ego, but I liked thinking maybe it was because of righteous indignation over what had happened to me. I didn't ask, because I didn't want to hear I was wrong. Either way, however, I was grateful. The beast inside was shrieking with the need to find the bad guys and tear people apart.

Sadie stayed with my new friends at the station, while the cops left to take care of our business. The FBI team went to a tattoo parlor I'd gotten the name of from Daniel, saying the backroom was a source of many dealings. It had apparently been where he'd done much of his work, and the magico-technic firewalls he'd set up had been run from servers there. It was within range.

Sam, me, and the PD team went to another warehouse on the other side of the arena building, although closer to it than the tattoo place. Both were in Adelheid's small 'industrial' area, which was mostly a few warehouses and very little actual industry, because preternaturals don't like smog.

The place was small. We approached it without the lights and sirens because we didn't want anyone to see us coming and hightail it. Vampires can hightail it better than most, after all. We parked at strategic spots around the block and slipped out of our cars. It felt good to be in my own clothes and wearing my bullet proof vest, gun in hand. Even if not all of me felt like it used to, this was familiar. Even if I didn't need the vest like I used to, it was still comforting.

Once all of the exits were covered, including officers watching the windows from the outside, Sam and I kicked down the door and streamed in. Now we were happy to make a racket, shouting our presence and strategically scouring the area.

"Vance," Sam got my attention and nodded to a set of metal stairs leading to an office suspended above us. Focusing my new superpowers, or the vampire senses at least, I could see shadows moving behind tinted windows. Arms were waving, and I realized I could hear yelling that was completely unrelated to us.

"I bet it's them," I said.

Guns at the ready in our perfect, textbook form, we moved forward and ascended the stairs. I reached the top first. I'd been faster than Sam before, and now that was even truer. I got to the door and kicked it off its hinges.

"Adelheid PD!" I shouted, not caring about the vampire volume.

The only two in the room were Conall and another male vampire I felt safe in assuming was Niall. The pair was so engaged in a screaming match with each other that they still were at it for several seconds after the door had gone flying across the room. I did have to admire their dedication.

"Adelheid PD!" Sam and I shouted again, in chorus.

The vampire brothers finally noticed and whirled on us. We all stared at each other for a moment before they turned and bolted. Niall elbowed his brother off course and reached the door in the back first. Sam was already on his heels, and I was after Conall. We chose our roles without having to consult. It was just instinct.

I barreled into Conall's back and sent him crashing into the wall. He spun on me with a dark smile.

"Why, Detective, there's something different about

you," he said.

"You're under arrest, Conall Blackwood." I didn't want to dignify him with a response. I kept my gun on him and began to advance. Focusing on doing my job helped to keep other, darker things at bay. I began to recite his rights because that also helped me focus.

The eldest Blackwood child, however, seemed to have no intention of going peacefully. He surged at me with a burst of vampiric speed. I had the same reflexes, but not the time to have gotten used to them. The gun was knocked out of my hand, but I grappled with him easily.

We exchanged a few blows, and my rage exploded. He was evil, but I was angry, and apparently that proved stronger because in my episode of blinding fury, I somehow got him on the ground. I was on top of him and didn't even know I was just beating the shit out of him until the haze of red passed.

And yet I didn't seem to care.

Thoughts careened through my head, seeing this as the man who had turned me into a murderer. Images of my fight with that female vampire flooded behind these thoughts. I saw her on the ground and heard the sound of her flesh tearing. It was like a roaring in my ears. The taste and smell and feel all combined, like I was in that moment again. But now it filled me with anger at the man who'd put us in that position...for *fun*.

This man had made me a most unwilling murderer, and in such a way that I was willing at that moment yet not in control. I had shredded another being so that he could bring in the money of people who wanted to *watch*.

Now I wanted to tear him apart, but this was justice. At least, that's what the sensation in my head was saying as I hit him and he could do little to stop me.

Until I heard a voice shouting my name and felt arms

pulling me back. I struggled at first, but I realized it was Sam. "He's not worth getting in trouble over, Vance," she was shouting in my ear. "Don't do this to Sadie!" I stopped struggling and looked down at the groaning vampire on the floor.

Once she felt certain I had stopped, Sam let me go and moved over to Conall, cuffing him with our very special cuffs. Even a vampire couldn't break through these.

I watched as she got him to his feet. He was still conscious and didn't really look as worse for wear as I would have expected, although there were several places where old blood oozed from his wounds. Older vampires were gross like that. (Something I had to look forward to now, I realized.)

Two uniforms came in and took Conall from her. I stayed sitting on the floor.

"Did you get Niall?" I asked.

"Yes." She sat beside me. "That wasn't good, Vance."

I sighed. "I know. I just..."

She patted my arm. "I know." She let out a breath. "Bad guy is in jail. We'll just say you got in a fight while apprehending him."

"It is the truth," I pointed out, leaning toward her but without meeting her eyes.

"We'll get the others, too." She sounded sure of herself, but I guessed that was a good thing. "And you, dude, I think you need to take a little time off."

CHAPTER SEVENTEEN

The big passenger plane sat on the tarmac of Bradley International Airport. Dots of light lined the night sky beyond the window as the plane welcomed the last of its passengers on board before shutting the door and setting off. The hum of people's conversation was a permanent dull murmur as flight attendants told people to take their seats and looked in overhead baggage compartments.

I was going on vacation. I figured I'd earned it. I didn't have a lot of choice either, because Sam insisted I take some time off to recover from my ordeal. Roy supported her choice, but I was fairly certain she hadn't mentioned my little lapse in control in that warehouse. And Conall had been mostly healed by the time anyone else had seen him, so point for me. Who was gonna believe the spawn of Satan over me, you know?

Whatever. No one ever said anything, except, "Geez, man, take some time off."

Sadie leaned her head against my shoulder, and I kissed her hair. "I can't believe," I began, "that after so many deca—"

"Hey."

"That after all this time," I amended myself, "you've never been to Las Vegas."

She shrugged. "I'm an east coast girl. What can I say?"

Chuckling quietly, I shook my head and leaned back in my seat.

We were on a night flight that would take us to Sin City for an extra-long weekend. It was a flight that had to be very carefully timed, what with the sun and all, but airlines were more accommodating of these matters nowadays. As much as airlines are ever accommodating of anything, really. And the days were still short enough to afford a wider margin of darkness. We'd get there in plenty of time.

So, how did it all roll out, I'm sure you're wondering.

Conall and Niall were being held in a high-security, magically-enhanced prison that was designed with vampires in mind. Conall wasn't talking, but he also wasn't trying to get police brutality charges on me either. Maybe he was embarrassed. I wasn't asking. His brother, on the other hand, was in talks with the feds to give up a lot of information for some kind of deal. I didn't know the details, and I wasn't planning to ask any time soon. It gave everyone hope that Alastair and Kenna would be brought in, however, although they were on the run now.

Even if we didn't get them, we'd at least be able to shut down a lot of the Blackwood Family stuff, if Niall was as cooperative as we hoped he would be.

For me, life felt really different and yet not that different at all. It was weird how that worked. I missed food, but there is no better sleep than a vampire day coma. The blood thing isn't so bad.

I got to keep my job, although obviously it was going to be a lot different now. I was just grateful I didn't have to quit.

Sadie was trying to talk me into seeing a shrink for the… temper issues I'd been dealing with since the arena. And the whole trauma angle. I wanted to just be a guy and not talk at all, but she was persistent. I agreed to start with Nykk and go from there.

"How about Elvis?" Sadie asked.

"How many times do I have to tell you?" I laughed. "We

are not getting married by Elvis, even if we are in Vegas!"

Oh, yeah. You hadn't guessed? We were eloping. There was going to be a bigger ceremony for friends and family in Adelheid in the summer, but after my near-death experience, I didn't want to wait that long to call her my wife. And we'd already had what I was calling the marriage by blood—the vamping thing. So, a long weekend getaway, get hitched, and then have the life I wanted. Sort of.

"Come on! Where's your sense of humor?" Madison tossed herself in the seat behind us after a steward told her she had to, but she leaned over the top. "Think about it. You're now, like, the most overpowered D-and-D character ever, so time to really live it up!"

My 'little sister' had sniffed out our plans (because we told her) and absolutely refused to be left behind. She threatened to pack herself in our suitcase if we didn't take her, so she was going to be our witness. And kicked out for much of the time since this was supposed to be our honeymoon. It didn't hurt that Chance, her sort of boyfriend, was temporarily living in Vegas. I didn't imagine she would mind being on her own and away from us.

Truth be told, I was kind of waiting for a pair of flies to land on my shoulder and turn into Dakota and Edward, but so far, that hadn't happened.

With Sadie's hand in mine, I idly played with her engagement ring. She didn't say anything, which I appreciated. Peace was something of a rare commodity for me since it had all happened.

My time inside those bars had been so short, but I would never be the same. That was taking some getting used to.

And if you're wondering about the others, Roy kept his word. I knew he would. They were free to return to their lives, although they were keeping in touch. I was going to have more friends than I knew what to do with. Hell, even Dakota had called me a couple of times to see how I was.

Shocking, right? I knew I must have been in bad shape if *she* was worried.

Still, I guess life can't be that bad. I have a lot of people who care about me, and that's what I ultimately learned in that hell hole. As cliché as it might sound, it all comes down to people. It's all about knowing that lives are valuable and that lives are *lives*, human or preternatural. We are not expendable. We are not dispensable.

We are not disposable people.

If you want to know more about the town of Adelheid, the people who live in it, and the lore I chose to use when writing these preternatural species, you can check out my series wiki at wiki.authorkbthorne.com.

ABOUT THE AUTHOR

Born a Connecticut Yankee in nobody's court, K. B. Thorne grew up to brave snow and talk fast.

She started reading when she was three and never looked back, soon frequently falling asleep with a book under her cheek. At eleven, she discovered *Night Mare* by Piers Anthony and entered the world of grown-up fantasy fiction. As you can guess, it was all over from there. She started writing at fourteen, then met vampires as a teenager and the concept for what would become Adelheid (now the Blood Rights Series) was soon born. Mia Darien followed a few years later, and the books were released.

However, K. B. is also a third-generation Trekkie. Somewhere in a vault at Paramount is a very angry letter written by her grandmother when *Star Trek: The Original Series* was cancelled, so sci-fi is in the blood too. Alongside a love of love and an adoration for her first love of epic fantasy.

K. B. Thorne is the evolution of Mia Darien after years of learning and living. She has taken both of those things to become a smarter, better writer with a fresh new face and take on the literary world. Thorne writes the urban fantasy, fantasy and sci-fi, while Sadie Johnston writes the romance.

These days, when she's not desperately trying to find time to write, she works as a freelance editor/cover artist/formatter and happily lives her unconventional life alongside her very own Named Man of the North and their mini-tank. (Who is, you know, their son.)

You can find K. B. at authorkbthorne.com!

Other Books
by K. B. Thorne

Writing as K. B. Thorne
Blood Rights Series

Bad Blood
Blood and Thunder
Blood Moon
Written in Blood
Bloodshot
First Blood
Out for Blood
New Blood
Flesh and Blood

Out for Blood Series
Bones & Blood

Bellator (Anthology)
Good Things (Anthology)
Ashes to Sunrise (Anthology)
The Shape of Tomorrow (Anthology)
Born of Defiance (Anthology)

Writing as Sadie Johnston (Romance)
Beauty
Help Wanted (with Viola Dawn)
Threnody (with Alastair Malone)
Here, Kitty Kitty (Anthology)
Amor Vincit Omnia (Anthology)
Second Chances (Anthology)

www.ingramcontent.com/pod-product-compliance
Lightning Source LLC
Chambersburg PA
CBHW020611160726
47991CB00002BA/730